Smokin
MIRRORS

BUILT ON *lies*,
DESTROYED BY THE *truth*...

A NOVEL BY
MIKE O.

Smokin Mirrors

By

Mike O

Publisher's Note

This is a work of fiction. Any names historical events, real people, living and dead, or the locales are intended only to give the fiction a setting in historic reality. Other names, characters, places, businesses and incidents are either the product of the author's imagination or are used fictiously, and their resemblance, if any, to real life counterparts is entirely coincidental.

Edited by: Darren Rochester

Proofreader: M. Dixon-Bey

DC Bookdiva Publications

#245 4401-A Connecticut Ave

NW, Washington, DC 20008

www.dcbookdiva.com

facebook.com/thedcbookdiva

Acknowledgements

I have to thank God first and foremost, always, and I have to thank him for my child for saving me from myself. I appreciate all those who supported my freshman project, 1000 Grams with 21st Publishing, and I want to say a special thank you to the online book clubs: Black Faithful Sisters and Brothers, Divas & Gents into Urban Lit, Black E book cub, Readers R Us, My Urban Books Club, Nook Readers, Let's Talk Relationships and Books,. Gotta thank the All4One Squad (Authors Promoting Authors). I really appreciate each and every person that has supported my writing career, and get ready cause I'm about to flood the market with titles. To my family, I love you ALL, and to my city, you know I'm Tre4 and I love my city!!!!!!!

And I have to give a special shout out to my girls Carla Towns and Sandy Thebookconnoisseur Barnett Sims for looking out for me!!!!!!!!!

Mike O

Find me on Facebook @ Thewriter Formerlyknownaz Mikeo

Follow me on Twitter @Mikeothewriter

Chapter 1

Chuck was in love the moment he laid eyes on her in 1992. He spotted her standing at the snack machine at Carver High School in front of the gymnasium. She was bent over, trying to reach her arm up through the bottom of the trap door to release the Snickers that was stuck in the machine.

"Need some help?" Chuck asked, while walking up and coyly admiring the roundness of her butt in the short shorts that barely concealed the crease between the booty and the back of her thighs.

"Oh, it's not what it looks like," Cynthia answered laughing while trying to wiggle her arm from the slot.

"Looks like you got yourself in a jam, so let me help you out." Chuck bent down on one knee and gingerly helped her release her hand. She smelled like fresh picked strawberries from a country farm.

Cynthia quickly stood up and began shaking her wrist trying to get the blood flowing again, causing her 34-C cup perky titties to bounce around like she was doing jumping jacks. Her 5'3" frame was perfectly constructed and had just enough meat to drive a man crazy, but not enough to be considered obese. She was thick, with silky looking skin that glistened from the Nivea lotion that she used daily. She had flawless legs with not a mark in sight, and her tiny cheerleader shorts hugged her hips and ass like a mother would hold her newborn baby.

"Here, let me show you how to do this," Chuck assured her while removing the black and white Major Damage button down shirt, leaving him in his crisp cotton wife beater. He gripped his hands on both sides of the machine and began to violently shake it.

Cynthia stepped back and proceeded to check him out, she loved the way his thick muscles curved as he shook the machine back and forth. He was fresh to death from head to toe, sporting a Damage outfit, and rocking a fresh pair of Nike Cortez to match the black and white pattern. His hair was cut in a Gumby style, with a part which started in the front and curved around towards the back of his head and eventually looped back around at the end. Chuck was definitely a fly guy, and something about him sent sensations shooting through Cynthia's vagina and up into her chest. His dark coffee complexion would nicely complement her rich butterscotch skin. She watched as the candy bar dropped from the evil clutches of the snack machine, while Chuck bent down to retrieve it. He turned around with a boyish smile.

"Here you go."

"I really appreciate that.

I don't know what I would have done without you."

"Ah, don't mention it," Chuck eagerly extended his hand to welcome Cynthia's palm.

"I'm Chuck, and you are?"

She studied his hands, and noticed how smooth they were, and placed hers into his. "I'm Cynthia, but everybody calls me CeCe."

"Well CeCe, I really like that pretty smile of yours!" Chuck flashed his own perfectly straight teeth;

which had a slight yellow tint from a smoking habit he picked up a couple years ago.

"Well thank you, but I have to get to practice." CeCe released Chuck's hand and turned to scurry away.

Chuck gently grabbed her arm, "Hey wait, you gotta boyfriend?"

CeCe took a few seconds to process the question at hand. The last five guys that put their hands on her wound up bent over grabbing their balls, but something about Chuck made her feel comfortable and safe. He seemed like the man of her dreams. His almond brown eyes had her in a trance for a while, and then she admired the curvature of his lips.

"Nah, I don't have time. With cheerleading and my studies, I barely have time for myself."

"Well do you think you can make time for a friend?" Chuck asked.

"Maybe, it depends."

"On?"

"On what a friend means to you, what do friends do? Speak and keep it moving?" she asked.

"Nah, friends are friends. They talk on the phone, hang out at school, sneak out to kick it, you know, whatever friends do."

"*Sneak out huh?*" CeCe thought; what should have been a red flag had her instantly intrigued. "Well, I don't know about that, but do you have a pen?"

"Is pig pussy pork?" He laughed and whipped out the Bic he stuck in his pocket earlier.

"Boy, you crazy." CeCe couldn't help but giggle at the remark.

"Hold out your hand." CeCe gripped his fingertips and scribbled her phone number down. "Here, make sure you don't lose it."

"Oh trust me, I won't. I'm gonna to guard it with my life!"

"With your life, it's not that serious."

"It is to me." He cracked a half smile.

CeCe was charmed by the debonair young man, and a smile came across her face. "Ok, so call me later, around 8. I have my own line, so I'll answer the phone. You won't have to worry about my parents."

"Aight, bet."

As her feet carried her away from his eyesight, Chuck watched her supple ass shake and jiggle, knowing that she was doing a little extra for him. He wanted her and was cursing himself for not meeting her earlier. He thought he knew every chick in the school, since he was a popular basketball player. As he re-dressed, he watched her disappear into the group of cheerleaders and he turned to leave. He stepped outside to howling winds and leaves rustling about while wishing his Triple Fat Goose wasn't stuffed in the backseat of his candy apple red 1990 Nissan Pulsar equipped with t-tops and black interior.

Walking swiftly to the car, he fumbled the key into the hole, and turned it to unlock the door.

"Yo, what's the deal blood?" T-Bone walked up from out of nowhere, followed by his right hand man Chico.

"Ain't shit blood. What's popping with you?" Chuck answered looking back over his shoulder as he grabbed his coat from the back seat.

"I know you coming to the meeting tonight, right blood?" T-Bone asked, while holding his head back to see clearly under the red bandanna.

"I don't know man, I got some…" Chuck tried to say, but Chico quickly stepped in and cut him off.

"Fuck you mean you don't know? We don't miss no meetings blood. You knew that before you got that ass beat to join this organization. The only way out is in a box, you ready to die blood?"

T-Bone and Chico were a deadly duo that migrated from Los Angeles, CA back in 1982, and moved to Winston-Salem. They began recruiting weak minded high school boys who yearned for a sense of belonging. They were at least 11 years their senior since they both were twenty-five. They mainly recruited boys fourteen and up.

Chuck first met T-Bone in an East Winston Burger King parking lot on MLK. He wasn't hard to spot either, dressed in a black Dickie suit with a red t-shirt and some black and red Chuck Taylor's. He topped the outfit off with a red bandanna that smothered his forehead. The ends of his hair dripped with Jheri Curl juice.

Chico was about 6'2" and hovered over T-Bone's 5'11" frame. Chico was a Mexican immigrant who crossed the border years ago and was determined to never return to Mexico or prison unless it was in a body bag. Chico was a hard core thug and really should have been the leader of the two, but T-Bone had the control.

"Man, I'm gon' be there, chill with the threats and shit bruh, cause I ain't scared of ya ass. We can scrap like a muthafucka right here." Chuck stepped up raising his voice looking Chico right in the eyes.

"Whoa, Whoa," T-Bone said calmly, pressing the cold steel barrel into Chuck's temple. "You need to stay in your place blood."

Chuck, knowing not to press the issue, but unfazed by the gun in his peripheral vision, let his hands relax and said calmly, "I will be there tonight bruh, believe that."

"Good." T-Bone tucked the pistol neatly in his waistband and the two men slowly walked off.

Chuck hopped in the car sniffling, his nose was beet red and his face felt like it would crack from the bitter cold and biting winds. He was starting to see that the two goons didn't belong around here. They had plenty of followers, but in this grimy city, they were still considered "Outta Towners." Outta Towners got dealt with when they stepped outta line, and this was their last straw.

Chuck looked at CeCe's number scribbled across his palm with a smiley face beside it. A smile crept across his face, as he grabbed a pen and piece of paper to transfer the number in case he washed his hands and forgot it was on there.

Chapter 2

Salt and Pepa's hit song "Push It" was blasting through the boom box as CeCe pranced around the room in her underwear. She was preparing her clothes for the next day of school; CeCe always kept the latest fashions. The soft scent of Dove soap lingered in the air from her hot shower. As she danced around admiring her shape in the mirror, the hamburger shaped phone on her pearl white dresser started ringing.

"Hello?" CeCe answered after killing the volume on the boom box.

"Hey"

"Who is this?"

"Your future."

"Oh yeah," she glared into her own eyes imagining Brett rubbing all over her body.

"Oh yeah, I'm glad you answered."

"Why wouldn't I answer silly? I always answer the phone when you call."

"Huh?" Chuck curiously looked down at the phone, hoping he had dialed the right number. "Is this CeCe?

"Duhhhhh, Brett what's wrong with you tonight?" she asked.

Chuck almost hung the phone up in anger, but remembered they had just met and he couldn't be angry. "This is Chuck; we met at school earlier today."

"Chuck?" CeCe belted, "Ohhhh, Chuck yeah I remember now. My bad, you sounded like someone else!"

"Brett right? Who is that? I thought you didn't have a boyfriend?"

"Ummm don't you think it's a little too soon to be asking me 20 questions? And Brett is not my boyfriend, just like you aren't, so I'd appreciate it if you don't question me again!"

Chuck gritted his teeth, but managed to say "My bad, I don't know what I was thinking. I'm kind of sleepy."

CeCe glanced at the clock on her night stand. "It's only 8:30, you about to go to bed this early?"

"Yeah, why not?" Chuck answered, but he wanted to tell her not to question him just as she had told him.

"No reason, I'm just up and I'm probably gon' read ahead for my History class. You know, get ahead of the game to keep myself up on the competition. Don't you do that?"

Chuck yawned, "Yeah I do, but I was just calling to check in on you and to let you know you had been running through my mind all day. I was trying to see if you needed me to massage those."

"Massage what? What are you talking about?"

"Nothing ma, I'm just gon' hit you up tomorrow."

"Ok, goodnight." CeCe hung up the phone pissed that he didn't answer her question. Since he reminded her of Brett, she figured she would give him a call.

****

Chuck placed the receiver down and took a deep breath. He had to push the conversation to the back of his mind so he could focus on the task at hand. The crisp night moon shined brightly overhead, only peeking ¼ of itself out on this freezing winter night. The howling winds outside rattled the windows of the project apartment's front room.

Chuck's mom was still at work, and he knew she would be home by 11:30. He had to be swift in his action; he didn't have all night to be bullshitting. As he sat gazing outside, three shadows approached the porch. From the way the tall slender figure bopped side to side, he knew it was Hakeem. The short stocky one on the right was Tony. The medium built Harold brought up the rear.

Hakeem tapped on the screen door three times, then opened it and walked in.

"What's up bruh?" He spoke in a deep voice, with a strong Louisiana accent; he was from the Pork and Beans projects in New Orleans.

"Ain't shit." He dapped Hakeem's huge hands, which they jokingly called monkey paws. When he whooped somebody, he made sure he pounded those concrete knuckles all in their grill.

"What up Tony, what up Harold." Chuck reached out slapping the two men five, "Ya'll ready to do this?"

The small, stuffy project living room was cluttered: there were blankets on the sofa, plates from yesterday's dinner, trash strewn across the floor, and roaches having a field day on the walls and scattered about like they paid rent. The food from yesterday was Chinese, and had the living room smelling like Mr. Lu's.

All three men smelled the stench but this was clean compared to their homes. Sunshine projects had been their home as far back as they could remember. Roaches and trash everywhere was as much a part of their lives as gunfire after dark. Their mothers were all too busy chasing the streets, getting high, and working. They barely cleaned up, and didn't care enough to pick up after themselves.

"Hell yeah, I'm ready, I been wanting to murk these clowns, woadie." Hakeem spoke. He was barely visible in the living room; as if his tar baby complexion wasn't enough, everyone was wearing all black. Hakeem had long thick dreads, which he had been growing since elementary school. Now that they were all seniors at Carver High, they had grown considerably.

"Good, let's roll," said Chuck. The four men exited the house, with a two hour window before their mothers got off at the local bakery.

****

"Aye holmes, tonight when that cock sucker Chuck shows up at the meeting, I wanna vote to have his ass murked. He's been too defiant recently." Chico expressed, as they rode in T-Bone's Toyota wagon. It had a lemon yellow paint job, deep dish hammers, and tinted windows; they were passing a blunt back and forth.

"Come on now Chico, Chuck been loyal to us since we ran into him in elementary school, and he's been like a bad ass lil brother to me. I don't see no reason to murk him," T-Bone responded.

"Shit, did you see the way he bucked at me earlier? This muthafucka's feeling himself now that he's older. He's gonna be a problem. I know you don't want that."

"You really think he's got the guts to go up against us, Chico? These country niggas know better. We started the Blood culture around here, and look how it's spread from hood to hood. In Winston-Salem, we like Tookie Williams and 'nem. We run this town."

"Yeah Bone, we been running the town for a while now, but you don't think one of these bumpkins wanna try us?"

"Not Chuck, he know better. Chill blood, everything gon' be 'aight. How about this, I'll let the two of you fight it out and you can whoop his ass and get him back in line. He has been smelling himself lately."

"That's what I'm saying holmes, I'm gon' pound his ass." Chico punched his fist into his palm as they were pulling into the driveway of the Trap House.

"Let's go chill until the meeting tonight."

T-Bone inserted the key into the hole and opened the door. He flicked the light on and hung his keys on the wall. The two men entered the house and looked around cautiously with their hands on their waistbands; all seemed normal. They were always extra cautious when entering and exiting the house. T-Bone made his way through the living room, while Chico went to the bathroom to take the piss he had been holding for the last ten minutes. Without even flicking on the light, he crammed into the tiny bathroom, lifted the seat and began to relieve himself.

Before he could finish, something familiar was jammed into the back of his neck, "Shit," he hissed, he knew what it was.

"What the fuck?" Chico questioned.

"Shhhh, this won't hurt at all." The voice assured him and whacked the pistol across the side of his face, making him see stars before he fell to the floor and passed out.

"What the hell was that?" T-Bone yelled out after hearing the thud in the bathroom. He got no answer. "What the fuck," he began reaching for his firearm as the pantry door flew open.

"Get the fuck on the ground, NOW!"

"Whoa, Whoa, just" T-Bone started, but was smacked in the face with the .40 caliber Glock, causing blood to pour down his face and flood his left eye.

"Shut the fuck up!" the voice behind the mask spat. His right hand came crashing down with the butt of the gun to the back of T-Bone's neck, sprawling him out on the dirty kitchen floor.

"You get that bitch ass nigga back there?" Chuck called to the back. His question was answered when Hakeem and Harold came out dragging Chico's arms, while Tony had his feet.

"What we gon do wit 'em?" Hakeem asked.

"Let's tie 'em both up to these kitchen chairs, sit 'em in the middle of the living room and get creative," Chuck responded.

"Wake the fuck up!" Hakeem dashed the kerosene in the face of T-Bone, causing him to stir from the burning sensation of the gas inside the fresh wound on his forehead.

"Mmmmm, mmmmm!" T-Bone tried to belt out, but found himself gagged and bound to the wooden chair. He looked beside him and noticed Chico's head hung to the side, he was still knocked out.

Hakeem changed that quickly as he dashed the kerosene in Chico's face, bringing him to life. As he came to, he noticed that the three other men were dousing the house with kerosene. His eyes became wide, and his heart tried to chisel its' way out of his chest.

"Yeah muthafucka, you were hard earlier huh," Chuck spoke in his regular voice peeling the mask from his face." "Yeah, it's me bitches. You two had to know I was getting tired of following ya'll around. Got me out here making scraps off the dope ya'll give me. Thinking I'm country and slow." Chuck stepped forward and slapped Chico upside the head with his glock.

"Yeah nigga." Hakeem piggy backed off his friend and slapped steel to T- Bone's head as well. "Man let me kill this piece of shit Chuck," he begged as he had the gun at point blank range ready to spill T-Bone's brains on the dingy beige carpet.

"Nah, that's too easy. We gon' burn these cock suckers alive. We didn't spend all that money on that fire retardant rope for nothing."

"Yeah you right woadie, plus the fumes in this bitch would set us on fire, and I damn sure ain't trying to die with these punks," Hakeem laughed.

Tony and Harold looked out the window to make sure they didn't get any unwanted company.

"So like I was saying, I'm tired of following you lames." Chuck glanced at the clock on the wall noting that they had 20 minutes to get home and in bed. "Well, let's go fellas." Chico glared at T-Bone with "I told you so," screaming from his eyes.

The four men prepared to leave the house, ensuring Chuck was the last to exit. He turned around and said, "Hasta lavista, baby!" then struck a match and tossed it. He watched as the flames begin to immediately engulf the living room. He smiled devilishly and exited the house.

T-Bone and Chico feverishly rocked back and forth trying desperately to free themselves from the restraints, as their muffled cries grew louder. They were fighting a losing battle and knew death was imminent. After all the years of putting in work, they had been beaten by a protégé. The room quickly morphed into a smoldering inferno, instantly separating flesh from bone. As the two burst into flames, the room was filled with the stench of burning human tissue.

Chapter 3

Brett lightly tapped on the window as CeCe seductively tip-toed over with a smile on her face. The powder blue silk nightie she was wearing was so thin that he could see she had on nothing underneath. She was ready to get hers tonight. She slid the window up as quietly as she could so Brett could squeeze his 5'9" frame through the small opening without making too much noise.

"Shhh," she put her finger to her mouth as he plopped on the floor, and she hurried to shut the window back.

"My bad," Brett whispered. The sound of his voice instantly soaked her clean shaven vagina.

Brett was everything she could ever want. He was walnut brown, with thick full eyebrows, and his lips curved and poked perfectly from his chiseled face. He was an All-American football player on the field, but to CeCe and many other teenage girls, he was Daddy Long Stroke.

CeCe was begging to give him some head, and was still a novice in the art, but Brett loved it. She may have used her teeth a little too much, but after a few ooh's and aahh's, she usually got the message. After she gave him head, she was ready to feel him inside her walls. "Fuck me baby," she whispered in a passionate tone. "Bend over," Brett said, he loved the way her ass jiggled when he hit it from the back.

CeCe loved the way he explored her insides, reaching new depths as he utilized every position-ultimately pinning her legs back and taking the straight approach to the bottom. Brett was killing the pussy tonight and CeCe could hardly contain her erotic moans, as he dug deep inside of her. They were in the throes of lovemaking and easily forgot that CeCe's grandmother was upstairs. Ms. White was awakened by faint whispers and light moans. "What the hell is that?" she asked herself. "That fast ass girl better not have no boy in this house," she said as she reached for her cane and climbed out of bed. She went to CeCe's room and tried to open the door, only to find out it was locked. "Heffa, you betta open this damn doe right now if you know what's good for ya," she yelled while banging on the door with her cane.

"Oohh shit," CeCe jumped while pushing Brett off her. She feverishly started searching in the dark trying to gather up her nightgown.

Brett hurriedly fumbled around in the dark for his clothes as well, but CeCe pushed him into the closet before he could grab his shoes.

"Coming Grandma," CeCe innocently said.

Brett listened as the door opened and the light flicked on.

"What were you doing in here?"

"Nothing Grandma."

"Then why you dressed like that?"

Caught off guard, she recouped quickly, "This was the only gown I had that was clean."

Brett listened to the two of them as Ms. White got closer and spotted the shoes. "Shit!" he said to himself, as the closet door flung open.

"I knew it! You got a boy in here! Get your ass out that closet right now!" she demanded.

Brett gingerly stepped from the closet, embarrassed that he had to meet her in this situation. CeCe's dad worked from 7PM-7AM, so he had dodged that bullet.

"Grandma... I." CeCe was interrupted when her phone smacked her head. Her grandmother was furious.

"*Damn!*" Brett thought and he wanted to buss out laughing, but kept a straight face. Then he felt her cane across his head, before Ms. White yelled "You betta get yo ass outta here before I get to my gun." Brett staggered out of the room and sprinted out of the house.

***

"Bomp, Bomp, Bomp," the alarm clock sang while Chuck reached up and fumbled to find the snooze button. The time read 5:30 AM, and it was time to get up and get ready for another day of school.

"Chucky, get yo lazy ass out that bed!" Sharon Jenkins yelled into his room from the hall. "Come on now, I'm making breakfast."

"Man damn," he spoke groggily, not wanting to get out of bed, but knowing his mother didn't play when it came to school.

Chuck stretched, placing his fist near his cheek and caught a strong whiff of kerosene emanating from his hand. The smell immediately woke him; he knew he had to get rid of it. He quickly hopped in the shower in an attempt to erase the incriminating evidence. The scorching hot water danced all over his Hershey chocolate complexion, as he lathered his body with the cheap Family Dollar soap. He felt good, smiling to himself as he ran his hands over his body until he reached his prized possession which dangled between his legs. This morning, his mind was still on CeCe and their conversation from yesterday.

He finished his shower, turned the water off, and reached out and grabbed his towel from the rack. He sniffed his hand and the smell was masked by the cheap soap. Satisfied, he draped his towel around his waist and stood in the mirror to brush his teeth. When he looked in the mirror, he didn't see a killer, he saw smooth ass Chuck. In his eyes, all the ladies loved Chuck.

He started getting dressed and noticed the smell of bacon frying, and he thought he smelled his favorite on the stove too. Fried potatoes and onions was his all-time favorite food; it was also easy to fix when his mom was on her crack binges.

"Smells good," he said as he walked into the kitchen confirming his suspicions. He admired the bacon, potatoes and onions, and eggs sitting in a bowl ready to be scrambled. Two pieces of toast sat stagnant waiting for Mrs. Jenkins to send them down after the eggs went on.

"Turn the TV to the news," Sharon commanded her son.

Sharon, back in the day, was beautiful. She was well proportioned with a nice firm ass and plump boobs. She had a shiny coco complexion with beautiful luxurious hair that bounced like the white woman's on the Head and Shoulders commercials. That all changed the minute she got her first hit of crack. Her breasts lost shape, and resembled soggy pancakes protruding from her boney chest cavity. Her booty looked like it had taken a vacation and vowed to never to return. Her skin went from clean and shiny to dirty, ashy, and black. The drug, combined with all the trials and tribulations she had been through with Chuck's father, David, left her hair salt and pepper.

David Jenkins was the man when she met him-he ended up being the worst thing to ever happen to her. He was the first person to get her to put that glass stem to her lips, and breathe in crack smoke. That smoke now infested her lungs and ran her life. One day David decided he couldn't take life anymore; he decided to blow his brains out at home. Chuck was only five at the time, and had the unfortunate task of discovering his father sprawled across the bedroom floor in a pool of blood. Seeing his father on the floor with brain matter scattered about the room didn't alarm him much. His first thought was, "I aint gotta worry about Daddy beating me no more." Seeing his father dead was the impetus that fueled his sickness.

"Want me to turn it up Ma?" Chuck called back over his shoulder to his mother who was putting the finishing touches on his breakfast.

"Yeah, so I can hear it."

Chuck slapped the side of the TV in order to get the picture to focus, and knocked the aluminum foil that hung on the antenna to the floor. He fumbled with the knob turning it slowly to increase the volume. The top story on the news popped up, and the scene was eerie. There was police tape around the house and it was totally black. The roof was caved in, and charred remains of wood barely held what was left together. It looked as if a strong wind could finish demolishing the flimsy home.

"Last night, a fire left two men dead. Foul play is suspected, as police say that the men were bound and tied to chairs in the front room. No suspects have been released at this time, but this gruesome murder scene marks the city's thirteenth homicide," the reporter stated while Chuck and his mom intently watched.

"This city is going to shit," Sharon said shaking her head. She placed the food on the table. "Come on, let's thank God for this food," she said as the two bowed their heads. Even though his mom was a crack head, she still loved the Lord.

****

"Man that's crazy," CeCe thought as she finished getting herself prepped for school while watching the news. She had to make sure her hair covered the knot on her head, and hoped and prayed her grandmother didn't tell her father about what happened last night. She knew he was going to flip!

She figured she would ride the bus to school this morning instead of her father taking her. She hurried from the house without breakfast, or money for lunch. She was scared that her dad was going to make her the city's fourteenth homicide.

The bell rang just as CeCe made it into the classroom, to sit in her boring ass History class. They learned about all kinds of events, but none of them interested her. She was more into what happened with black people versus what they teaching in these history classes. Even though she didn't like the subject matter, she was a straight A student. CeCe always excelled in her studies and was determined to leave high school, go to college, and become a dental hygienist. She already had her life and career goals mapped out.

After the teacher almost put her to sleep with his lecture, the bell finally rang. She was surprised she even heard it over her the sounds of her stomach rumbling. She headed to the snack machine in front of the gym on the second floor. Once at the machine she fumbled through her purse looking for money, but forgot that she rushed from the house trying to elude her father. That proved to be costly now, *"Damn, its gon' be a LONG day,"* she thought.

"Shit!" she blurted out, frustrated and hungry.

"I didn't think you knew words like that," Chuck said as he came walking up.

"Oh my bad, I just wanted a Snickers to hold me over til' lunch, but I realized I don't have any money today."

"You seem to like milk chocolate, packed with nuts." Chuck stated really talking about his Snickers he couldn't wait to pack inside her.

"I do, king-sized! These only hold off the hunger leaving me wanting more," she said as she licked her lips and pointed to the Snickers in the machine.

"You won't be left hungry, believe that." Chuck reached in his pocket and pulled out a wad of money. He flipped through the 100's, 50's and 20's to get to a dollar buried underneath all the heavy artillery. "Here," he handed her a dollar bill.

Now usually a dude pulling out a stack of money like that wouldn't faze CeCe, but it was just something about Chuck that wet her panties. Brett was good at digging her out, but he didn't have much of a future

ahead of him.   Brett was always in trouble, and
fighting. Since she knew nothing about Chuck, she
didn't wanna place a label on him.

"Thanks!"

"Don't mention it. Listen, if you free for lunch, I
can take you to get something."

"You drive?"

"Of course I drive. I wouldn't have a pocket full of
money and be walking. That would be hustling
backwards."

"Oh, you hustle?"

Chuck looked at how her expression changed and
answered, "Nah I cut grass for one of my mom's
friends. He has his own lawn care service."

"You mean to tell me that you made all that from
money cutting grass?" her lips curved up in disbelief.

"I'm not telling you anything else until lunch. It's
time for class. Meet me back here and we out. You
know what this may just become our spot," he smiled.

"I'll be here, and I'm starving so don't be late."

****

The bell rang and Chuck hurried to the spot so he
could take CeCe to lunch. He ran from one end of the
third floor to the other, jumping down steps and
dodging students to get there. When he finally made it,
he noticed that she wasn't there yet. He waited patiently
for her to show up, looking down at his gold nugget
watch.

"Waiting for me?" CeCe emerged from the gym doors unexpectedly.

"Yeah, you know I am. What took you so long? I thought you were hungry?"

"I am hungry, but I had to talk to my teacher after class. You ready?"

Chuck soaked her looks in. She was looking extra sexy in those tight acid wash jeans with random holes, yellow shirt with matching yellow leggings, and some black and yellow Fila's with the yellow fat laces. Her big bamboo earrings that said 'CeCe' and her assortment of little chains and bracelets let him know she was definitely fly.

"Hell yeah I'm ready," he answered the opened the door. "After you my dear, Chuck said in a fake British accent."

When the cold air swooped in, it made CeCe tug at her Member's Only jacket. "Damn its cold outside," she said walking out the door.

"Don't worry about it, I'll warm you up."

Chuck opened his Triple Fat Goose and snugly tucked CeCe inside as they walked to his car. He always smelled good, regardless of the way his house smelled and looked. The scent of Aspen cologne hugged his Notre Dame sweatshirt and the smell of CeCe's mushroom hairstyle reminded him of a salon.

When they reached the car, he had to remove her from his coat to stick the key in to unlock the door. He opened the door and made sure she was safely inside, then retreated to the driver's side. He smiled as she reached over to unlock his door for him.

"Let me hurry up and get this thing started," he said while jumping in and closing the door quickly behind him.

"Yeah it's freezing!" CeCe barely got out between chattering teeth.

"Here," he removed his coat, draped it across her, and started up the car.

"Thank you! You are so sweet. I wonder why I've never met you."

"Well you don't know every kid that walks by, do you?"

"You got a point there."

"I got more than that, for you."

She smiled then reached down beside her left leg. "You got a car phone?"

"You see it don't you," he smiled.

"Yeah I see it, does it work?"

"What kind of question is that?"

"You know these dudes be rocking beepers that don't work, stuntin and frontin."

"Well I don't stunt or front. You wanna make a call?"

"Nah, I don't have anybody to call."

"You got me."

"Yeah but you right here."

"I know, but it feels like a dream being next to you. Pinch me so I know it's real."

"Ok," CeCe reached over and pinched the shit out of Chuck.

"Ouch! Damn, did you have to try and kill me?"

They both laughed then headed out to get lunch. Since Carver was close to East Winston, Chuck figured the two of them could grab a bite to eat at Burger King. Pulling into the parking lot gave him a flash back of T-Bone and Chico, but he shook it off quickly and focused on the task at hand, CeCe.

Once they ordered he had her to take a seat in the booth while he made their drinks and fetched the condiments and napkins. After it all was taken care of, he sat down and began to dig into her brain.

"So, tell me something about you that you think I should know."

"What you wanna know?" she spoke trying to cover her mouth.

"I don't know, whatever you want me to know."

"Well it's not really much to tell. I'm a simple girl."

"You don't look simple." he motioned to her neck and wrist.

"My dad buys me all this stuff. And what he won't buy, my grandma will buy for me."

"I can't take your dad's place." he popped a french fry in his mouth.

"Nobody can take his place. Besides, he's the only man that I need to take care of me. My daddy told me he was gon' treat me how a lady should be treated, and he loved my momma to death." Her eyes welled up with tears.

"Where's your mom?"

"She died a couple years ago. She had cancer. My dad stayed by her side until she took her last breath. That's the kind of love I want, the kind I can take my last breath with."

"Sorry to hear that. That's deep though, so why are you single?"

"Cause dudes play too much, and I don't have time for that bullshit."

"You mean you really don't have anybody? What's that knot on your head?" Chuck asked noticing the lump protruding from her forehead.

"Oh this, I hit my head last night. And no I don't have anybody," she lied.

"Word, you need to be more careful. So, (he took a deep breath) I want us to start going out."

"What's going out?"

"You know, hanging out, me picking you up, maybe dishing out Snickers for you at lunch."

"Oh yeah," she burst out in laughter. "I like you Chuck. I can definitely get to know a guy like you."

Her words created a smile that the devil couldn't chisel away. They sat and talked more, and they laughed and joked until it was time to get back to campus. Their conversations had them both open. They were really digging each other, and only time would tell what the future held for the two. For now, they were happy being in each other's presence.

Chapter 4

Brett was outside when they pulled up in the school parking lot. CeCe never expected him to be there. Brett and his boys were standing outside near the gym battling in a cypher. CeCe's stomach dropped and she had to think quickly before Chuck parked and she had to get out and walk past Brett.

"Hey, since you being so nice you think you can drop me off around back? I left something in class."

"I would drive you to your class if I could," Chuck smiled.

Every time he smiled, it made her feel all warm and fuzzy inside. She really needed to wear a panty liner when she was with him; he kept her juices flowing. She just hoped he didn't have a teenie weenie stick between his legs. She couldn't deal with Vienna sausages when her pussy throbbed for a hunk of man meat.

"Here you go," he pulled up to the door smiling.

"Thanks, I really appreciate everything you've done for me today. See you after school?"

"No doubt! Same place?"

"No doubt," she answered and got out of the car. CeCe was so high off life that she didn't notice that Brett had spotted her and was angrily watching her walk into the building.

****

"Yoooo, that's that dude Chuck with your girl!" Eric said holding his fist up to his mouth.

"Shut the fuck up!" Brett spat back.

"Ain't no way I can let that shit ride. I would be whooping his ass soon as he walked up here," Josh readily added.

"Yeah, fuck it lets' beat his ass," Byron threw his two cents in.

Brett, Eric, Josh and Byron were all from The Hole, and they all were borderline crazy. They didn't come from broken homes, but they were just as bad or worse as the kids who did. Brett was the leader of the pack and the rest were followers. Eric was short and stocky. He was dark skinned and sported an afro; he kind of resembled the fat kid Steel from the movie Juice. Josh, on the other hand, was the total opposite-tall, yellow, with curly hair. He was a true menace to society. Byron was definitely the muscle out of the four boys. He played linebacker for the football team and was cock diesel. The ladies loved his dark complexion and big muscles.

They all watched Chuck park his car and step out with a glow like he just had the best time of his life. Brett was fuming on the inside. Chuck, unaware of the situation, noticed how he was being grilled by the four dudes standing outside.

"What ya'll niggas looking at?" He turned around to make sure he was the only person out there.

"Tha' fuck you mean what we looking at?" Byron spoke first.

"Oh word, you gon' try to flex? Ya'll must not know who I am?"

Rather than entertain what he was saying, Brett stole off on Chuck immediately. The first blow caught him by surprise, but he threw a right hand to Brett's jaw letting him know that this fight was going to be painful. As Chuck stepped back to square up with Brett, Byron released a hay maker that sent him stumbling to the ground. As soon as he hit the ground he saw Timberlands and Nikes fly in from all angles, immediately followed by fists. He knew he was done, until he heard the voice of his savior.

"Hey, break that shit up!" Officer Stokes belted. Brett and his crew took off running.

"Son, you okay?" he ran over to the helpless student's side.

"Yeah, I'm okay," Chuck grunted.

"Do you need medical attention?"

"Nah, I'll be alright."

"Here, let me help you up," Stokes extended his hand to him.

Chuck reached out and grabbed the officer's strong hand to pull him up.

"Who did this to you?"

"I don't know those dudes," Chuck lied because he definitely knew Eric's fat ass.

"Well come on with me to the office so you can make a statement, and we can get to the bottom of this."

"Nah, I'm good. I'm just about to go to class. I appreciate your help officer," Chuck said and quickly walked off. He didn't have any idea why those dudes were so stupid; he just knew that the situation wasn't over.

****

"CeCe!!!" Brett yelled from behind as soon as she left from her class.

"What's up? Why are you outside of my class, and why do you look like that?"

"We need to talk, Brett gritted."

"Ok, so talk"

"Not here, come and take a ride with me."

"Why Brett? You stalking me after my class, talking about we need to talk. I'm about to go home, school is over," she pointed up and down the halls. "Everybody is going home. Just call me later."

Brett's nostrils began to flare and he clenched his teeth, you could tell from the skin rippling at his temple that he was extremely upset.

"Bitch, how the fuck you gon' play me and be with that nigga Chuck earlier?"

CeCe had to make sure she was hearing him correctly. She had to circle back around to the first word.

"Did you just call me a bitch?"

Before she could get her next batch of words out of her mouth, he let it fly. He slapped her so hard that she fell to the ground. He cocked his foot back and gave her a hard kick in the stomach, forcing her to gasp for air.

"Don't fucking lie to me, I saw you bitch," he spat. Then he kicked her in the stomach again, but her arms shielded the force of the blow.

Realizing that he was wrong, he looked around and noticed a female student screaming and running towards them yelling "Stop!!!! Help!!!"

He took off running from the school through the back door to flee the scene. CeCe lay on the ground trying to regain her breath while feeling intense pains in her stomach. She could only curl up and cry, and listen to the voice say "Are you okay, Oh my God! Let me go get help." She heard footsteps running up the stairs and was left lying in the hall alone.

The young girl ran frantically and called out to the first person that she saw. "Come and help! A girl was just beaten downstairs. Go help her and I'm going to run to the office."

Chuck was concerned while he sat waiting on CeCe to meet him. He was packing heat in case he ran into more trouble. He wasn't trying to get another beat down. "*I need to get the fuck out of here,*" he thought to himself. But something inside of him told him he needed to see what was wrong. He went to the car to tuck the gun away, and grabbed a pair of brass knuckles instead. He stuck a knife in his pocket too.

Officer Stokes and the principal knelt down asking CeCe what happened, but she wouldn't move from the fetal position. Stokes jumped on the CB on his shoulder and called for an ambulance while they comforted her.

"CeCe!" Chuck called out when he saw her. He ran over to the scene to check on her.

"Whoa! Stay back!" Stokes belted.

Chuck ignored that. "That's my girl right there! What you doing to her? What happened?"

"Sir, I found her like this. She won't tell us what's wrong." The principal responded.

"Chuck, don't leave me," CeCe faintly whispered, indicating that she was in major pain.

This was too much for Chuck to absorb, and he was having feelings that he had never felt before. *Why was he so concerned with her wellbeing? Why was he in pain because she was in pain? Was it the way she smiled when they first met?* He couldn't fathom why he was having these feelings; he just knew he had them.

"I'm not leaving. I'm right here with you baby," he said as he affectionately looked down at her.

He heard sirens blaring in the background and they clouded his thoughts. *Damn, I hope she's gonna be okay. Should I go to the hospital with her? Who did this to her?* These questions were circling his mind. He killed those thoughts and decided that he was going to stay by her side.

****

"Where's my daughter?" the tall, handsome, light brown skin man asked at the nurse's station.

"Sir, what's your daughter's name?" the nurse asked.

"Cynthia White."

"And you are?"

"Her father!" he said starting to lose the patience that he came in with.

"Sir," he heard a voice behind him and turned around. "CeCe is your daughter?"

Vernon White looked Chuck up and down, and answered, "How do you know my daughter? And why are you here? Did you have something to do with her being here?"

"Sir, the doctor would like to speak with you over there." The receptionist interrupted, and pointed to where a tall, thin, white man in a white coat was waving a clip board.

Vernon took one more look at Chuck and said, "You stay right here. I have more questions for you," and took off towards the doctor.

The two men shook hands, "How are you?" the doctor asked.

"I'm not doing too well, my baby girl is here and I don't know what's going on. You care to share with me how she's doing?"

"Well sir, it appears the blunt force trauma caused your daughter to have a miscarriage."

"What?" Vernon's heart dropped to the pit of his stomach.

"Yes, she lost the baby. She should be fine in just a little while. The police want to know what happened, but she refuses to talk. There is a huge hand print on her face and I'm guessing she had to be kicked in the stomach. I'm just speculating; I don't know for sure. She's in that room." The doctor pointed to room 125. "But try not to get her too upset. She is heavily sedated, but stable. We'll be keeping her overnight."

"Thank you doctor," Vernon shook his hand, swallowed hard and walked toward the room.

"I can't believe this is happening to me, how am I going to tell my dad this?" CeCe thought while lying

up in the bed. Suddenly she heard a knock at the door and saw it open.

"Hey Pumpkin, can I come in?" Vernon nervously asked.

"Daddy!" she said in an excited tone. She had an IV dripping all the best pain-killers on the market through her veins.

Seeing his daughter like this, with the beeps of the machines made his eyes fill with a tears; something he hadn't done since her mother died. His baby girl was lying in a hospital bed. She looked exactly as her mother did when she spent her last days in a bed like this.

He pulled a chair up, slid it to her side, and took a seat. He grabbed his daughter's hand carefully; he didn't want to disrupt the needles that ran from her veins into tubes linked to the bags of medicine. He stroked her hand gently and his mind took him back......

****

"Hey Honey, how you doing today. I brought you something." Vernon held up the bouquet of flowers to show his wife.

She lay in the bed looking like a shell of her old self. Her body was so frail now; she was so voluptuous just a few months back. She was the best wife in the world to him and now here she was, waiting to die.

"I love them baby," Tonya spoke faintly, forcing her facial muscles to produce a smile. She loved her husband very much, and even on her death bed she would do anything to ensure he was happy.

He pulled up a chair and grabbed her hand. "I missed you today baby. How are you?"

"I'm tired baby."

"Well, you get some rest"

"Not that kind of tired, I feel myself about to leave this earth. I have made my peace with God, and I have spent my life making you happy. I love you and CeCe with all of my heart. Where is she?"

"I don't know, that girl of yours' is something else. Like mother, like daughter!"

She smiled slightly and gave a half laugh. "I had her with the best man in the world. I'm going to rest now Baby. I love you always," she said as she lay on her back and closed her eyes.

Tears streamed down his face, and for the first time he felt like his life was falling apart. He looked at the monitors and watched as the breathing rate declined. "Come on baby, fight!" he screamed, but her mind was already made up. She stopped breathing at 6:45PM and the monitor beeps went from various sounds, to monotone, then finally to a flat line.

****

"Daddy, are you okay?" CeCe asked, concerned about her father because he hadn't said a word.

"Yes Baby, I'm okay. How are you feeling?"

"I feel ok, I'm sorry Daddy." A tear escaped her eye but her father wiped it with his thumb.

"It's okay Baby, at least you're fine. This wasn't your time to have a child. You have your whole life ahead of you. A child right now would have been detrimental and I hope that this is a wakeup call for you. Your grandmother told me what happened last night, so I knew you were having sex. I really hate that we had to have this conversation like this."

"Daddy, I...." she started.

"No, wait, now before you say anything else, and please don't feel like you have to lie to me. You can tell me anything Pumpkin. Have I grown that distant from you that we can't talk? Don't you trust me?

"Yeah Daddy, I trust you."

"Well tell me what happened to you," he said.

CeCe sighed, "The guy who was at the house last night saw me with another guy at lunch today. He waited 'til after school to confront me and he hit me, and kicked me in my stomach."

"What's his name?"

"Brett, Brett Wallace. He lives in The Hole."

"Ok baby, you get some rest. I'm going to share this information with the police. Who is that other guy- he was dark-skinned, kinda tall, and had on a Notre Dame sweatshirt?"

"How do you know that Daddy?"

"He's out there in the waiting room. I have to go apologize to him for being so rude. I blamed him for you being here. I guess he really likes you; it looks to me like he's been out there waiting since you've been here. I'm going to send him in, and let him keep you company until I get back. I'll be back soon. I'm going to talk to the police," he gave her a kiss on the forehead before he left the room.

****

"Hey young man," Chuck heard a voice that startled him-but he recognized it.

"Sir?"

"She's in room 125, and she's waiting on you," Vernon told him. "Oh and make sure you take care of my daughter."

"I will sir."

"Go now, don't keep her waiting."

Another knock at the door startled CeCe again. The face that peeped in caused her heart rate to increase, and the biggest smile ever to appear on her face.

"Chuck," she spoke softly.

"Hey you, how are you feeling lady?"

"I'm feeling better. Thanks for coming; this really means a lot to me. You really didn't have to do this."

"Yeah, I know I didn't, but I wanted to. I had a conversation with you at Burger King and was really looking forward to seeing you again. I was posted up in front of the gym waiting for you when a girl ran from downstairs and said some female had been attacked, I had to come see if it was you."

"I was down there, on that floor, and I felt so alone. I was hoping you were going to save me. I almost gave up because it took you so long to get there. I was praying that you were upstairs and the one she called too. What took you so long though?"

This was that moment of truth that all men faced, when he chose a second half. *"Do you build a foundation on lies, or do you tell the truth?"* is the question that came to mind before he spoke. "Well earlier after I dropped you off, this fat dude named Eric and his homeboys jumped me; the same ones that were standing outside when we pulled up at school. You had your eyes on me, and I had my eyes on them. So after I dropped you off, I grabbed my pistol and tucked it in my waist," Chuck explained, but was interrupted.

"You have a gun? Why are you riding around with guns? Are you a gang banger?"

CeCe was getting turned on by the fact that Chuck had some thug in him. Good girls liked bad boys, and this mysterious creature in front of her really consumed her interest. She always looked at herself like a ride or die chick, and she needed a ride or die type of man.

"I'm not gon' lie to you; I used to be in a gang, but all that is dead," he started. He was referencing the fact that the originators of the Bloods were burnt to a crisp on some autopsy table. "I'm on some other shit. I'm tryin' to be successful."

"Doing what?" CeCe asked.

"I really wanna rap, but I'm cool with a regular job. I guess I could get out and get one."

"What about school? Do you plan to go to college?" she questioned.

"Well, I was thinking about that, especially since I'm a senior this year. I feel like I might need some time off. Maybe I'll go to school in a year. What you think?

"I think that would be cool. You can work and stay here with me. I don't graduate til' next year, so you can just get a job and wait for me to finish. We can fill out applications together and see where we get accepted. Maybe even go off together for college," CeCe responded. She had no idea where these plans were coming from. They had just met, but for some reason it was love at first sight.

Chuck had never planned for anything in life. He had always been a go-getter. Wake up in the morning, wash his ass and brush his teeth, then get to the money. He carried a pistol and a mentality that plagued young black men in America. He hated people of the same color, and the music that he loved glorified that hatred. In the end, he was all about the money. Money over everything!

Something about CeCe made him feel like she could be his Bonnie; he played Clyde's role perfectly. He had to scour around in his mind for answers before he said the wrong thing.

"That sounds like a plan to me. I'm really feeling you. Don't know what it is about you, but I would love to keep you by my side. Do you believe in fate?"

"Yes, I believe in fate. Do you think our meeting was fate?"

"It must be, why else would I be here?"

"You're right," CeCe smiled. She then asked, "Was my Daddy still out there talking to the police?"

"What police? I overheard the officer telling the doctors that they were going to let you rest, and they would be back tomorrow to talk to you."

CeCe wore a puzzled look; her dad told her he was stepping outside to talk to the police. "So where did he go?"

Chuck shrugged, "I don't know. He told me to make sure I take care of you and he left."

"I wonder where he went...."

Chapter 5

The car pulled up to the White home and Vernon lethargically switched the ignition off. His thoughts were focused on his CeCe while she laid in a hospital bed. She was there because of an abusive teenage boy who decided to put his hands on her. That boy was Ben Wallace's son.

Ben and Vernon knew each other from growing up in Winston-Salem in the 70's. In high school, they were once considered rivals. They wanted the same girls, always tried to outshine each other, and Vernon was the starting point guard on the basketball team. Ben was his back-up and desperately wanted to be the starter. The two men never had a physical confrontation, but it was obvious that neither of them liked the other. They were both always respectful in their quarrels and neither of them would ever lay a hand on a woman. They came from an era when men respected women.

"It's that damn rap music," Vernon thought aloud. He was trying to rationalize why so many of the young men these days were hitting women. He seethed with anger because this time, his child was the victim.

When the thought of a helpless CeCe being brutally attacked popped into his mind, he opened the car door and stepped out to endure the brisk cold winds. He marched into his home and went directly to his room. He slammed the door and plopped on the end of the bed. He placed his face in his hands and began sobbing uncontrollably. He felt that men were allowed to cry as long as it was not done in public. Everyone was not worth your tears, in his mind, and some people viewed them as a sign of weakness.

Vernon's mind had already decided Brett Wallace's fate. He pulled himself together and stood in the mirror with murder in his eyes. He wanted revenge so bad that he could taste the sweetness. He refused to go to sleep knowing that this monster was out there and could harm his baby girl again. He reached over into the nightstand and grabbed the .357 chrome snub nose revolver. He released the cylinder, and slid each bullet into place. His thoughts were with CeCe and the grandchild he would never get the chance to meet. He did not condone his daughter having a child at sixteen, especially while she was doing so well in school and had such a bright future. However, that was a choice that father and daughter would have had to make. Since Brett decided to play God, Vernon felt like it was time for him to get in the game. He took care of his family and there was absolutely no way was he going to let Brett hurt his daughter again.

****

Brett finished up his basketball game at the Carl Russell Recreation Center, dapped his boys up, and headed home before his mom got off work. Recently they had been at odds about Brett getting his life together. In his fourth year of high school, he didn't have enough credits to be considered a senior. The cold night air nipped away at the exposed skin under his toboggan. He wrapped up in his Chicago Bears Starter jacket as he walked from the rec back to the hood. The music from the new 2 Live Crew cassette tape was blasting in his ear. "One and One, we having some fun in the bedroom all day, and all of the night," Brett sang along as the distance home shortened with each step. As he was turning from Carver Rd. onto Butterfield Dr., a white Chevrolet Camaro that was leaving the hood slammed on brakes and screeched to a halt. Brett had no idea who was in the vehicle, and he peeled his headphones off as the car's window began to roll down.

"Ain't your name Brett Wallace?"

"Yeah that's me, why what's u…" was all he managed to get out as the first .357 slug pierced his chest cavity, splitting him open and sending him plummeting to the ground. Two more shots quickly followed, one to the abdomen and another to the groin. He was hit three times in less than 3 seconds.

Brett could hear the tires squealing as the car sped away. The bullets were burning his insides and blood spewed from his mouth. He rolled over to his side, and managed to utter his last words, "Oh God." His lungs collapsed and his heartbeat slowed immediately after. A loud ringing sound filled his eardrums as he looked ahead hoping and praying that these would not be his last breaths. He struggled and did all he could to cling to life, but within two minutes he was gone.

****

"Well, I'm going to get out of here so I can get some rest and I can get back here to see you first thing in the morning. It's getting late; you need to get some rest yourself. You need anything before I go?" Chuck asked while still holding CeCe's hand.

"No, I'm fine now. I think I could use some rest after all the shit I went through. I really appreciate you being here with me," she replied.

"Don't mention it." Chuck stood and delivered an erotic kiss on CeCe's forehead. "See you in the morning."

"Thanks again, see you in the AM. How early are you coming?"

"I should be here around seven. I'm gon' play hooky from school tomorrow, so when my mom wakes me up I'll just leave and come here. You want me to bring you some breakfast?"

"Sure, what did you have in mind?"

"I love Bojangles' breakfast. Their steak, egg and cheese biscuits are the bomb."

"That sounds good to me."

"Aight, I'll see you then."

Chuck slipped outside the room and decided he needed to go pay Eric and his boys a visit in The Hole. He felt they couldn't have thought about what they were doing earlier, but it didn't matter; it was payback time.

"When the fire dies down, what the fuck you gon' do, Damn it feels good to be a gangster!" Chuck sang along as the 10" subwoofers in the tiny trunk space pumped the new Ghetto Boys single. He had a .45 in

his lap, and was ready to put in some work. As he
approached Butterfield Dr., the scene caused him to hit
the mute button, stash the gun under his seat, grab his
seatbelt, slow down and pray that this wasn't a license
check.

Blue and red lights lit up the streets like the Las
Vegas strip. This street was usually dark, as was the
case in most low-income neighborhoods. Street lights
were few on this side of town.

Chuck followed the officers lead to go around the
traffic while keeping his eyes glued to the unfolding
site. The officer waved the orange cone shaped light to
snap him out of a daze, but he was still curious. The
next street on the right was Pressman Dr. and he made a
right and parked on the side of the street. The black
hoodie he wore came in handy as he pulled the hood
over his head and hopped out the car to take a stroll past
the crime scene. The yellow tape blocked the streets
and the detectives were scouring the scene making
marks on the pavement. The white bloody sheet over
the body told the tale. Somebody got murked.

"Hey, what happened?" Chuck asked a neighbor
who lived in the house facing the scene.

"Some boy got shot out here. I was inside cooking
when I heard three shots and then tires squealing. I
didn't see what kind of car it was though," the lady
explained. She was already used telling her story to the
police; they had already asked her a few times to tell
them what she knew.

"It was Brett mom! The dude that got killed was
Brett," the young boy who looked to be about ten,
blurted out. "I went and looked at him. He had blood

and stuff coming out of his mouth and his eyes were open. It was gross," he said with a frown.

"Thanks for the information ya'll, and lil man don't let that be you when you grow up. That right there," Chuck pointed to the location of the body, "that can happen to anybody. You better stay in school and follow the right path."

"I am! I love school, and I'm gon' be a doctor when I grow up."

"That's right Junior," the lady said embracing her son and kissing his head. "Thank God my baby got his head together; what about you young man?" she sprung on Chuck as he started to walk away.

"I'm about to graduate this year, and me and my girl got plans to get out of here and go to college."

"Know what you going to college for. Don't just go and get a degree only to be on the unemployment line like me. Research your options, and choose a good career."

"Ok ma'am, thanks. Y'all take care," Chuck said on his way back to the car. The good advice that the lady blessed Chuck with went in one ear and out the other. He was coming to kill people himself, so he definitely didn't practice what he preached.

Once he got back to his car, he decided that he would take it in. It was almost time for his mom to come home and he wanted to get in the bed before she got there. She would get off work with her lil crew and the first thing they did was drink and hit the local crack spot. She always came home wasted, and would start cooking. Like most crack heads, she never had an appetite. When the food was done, she would leave it out and head off to her room. Usually she was not alone and had one of her bruhs, as she called them, with her. However, the sounds Chuck heard through the walls didn't say bruh.

Young Chuck had to survive anyway he could. He always pretended to be asleep when his mom came in cooking and entertaining her company. They were always loud. Chuck would keep his head underneath a pillow trying to ignore his mom's annoying shriek laugh. As soon as she was done cooking and in her room with her company, Chuck would sneak in the kitchen and make a plate before the roaches had their feast.

The house was usually filthy. Most of the time she didn't clean up at all, but on random occurrences she turned into an OCD lady and would wipe the entire house down. That didn't seem to matter to the roaches though, they were always there. They were roaming around regardless, and they didn't scatter when the lights came on.

Chuck parked the car and went into the house to catch the late news. He wanted to see what was really popping. He heard the lil boy say Brett, but he had no idea who he was? The news would lay the story out. He picked up the remote, flicked on the TV and plopped down on the couch. He jumped back up to grab the newspaper off the flimsy front room table to kill a roach on the T.V. screen.

"Tonight, a young man was gunned down right here at the corner of Butterfield Dr. and Carver Rd. Seventeen year old Brett Wallace was killed." A picture flashed on the screen and Chuck blurted, "Oh Shit!" while breaking into a chuckle. "Neighbors say that the murder happened so quickly that they didn't see anything. There were some that reported hearing gun shots and tires screeching. Currently police have no leads on this case, this mark the city's fourteenth homicide this year.

"That's what he get," Chuck said and flicked the station off. He proceeded to get ready for bed so he could get back to CeCe.

Chapter 6

CeCe cracked her eyelids at 5:30 AM when her nurse knocked politely before she entered the room. "Good morning, how are you feeling?" the nurse asked.

"I'm fine. I'm kinda thirsty though. You think I can get some Ginger Ale?"

"Sure, let me just take a look at your blood pressure and make sure you're ok. The doctor will be releasing you this morning as long as the tests come back normal," the cute caramel colored CNA said. She placed the cuff around CeCe's upper arm and begin to pump. After slowly releasing the air and listening to her heartbeat through the stethoscope the nurse said, "Everything looks good; let me go get your soda."

After the nurse left, CeCe sat her bed in the upright position and flicked on the TV. She couldn't find anything to interest her, so she parked the station on Channel Twelve to catch the news. The nurse came back with her soda and she watched the screen as she sipped. When the top story aired she noticed the Butterfield Dr. sign and said to herself, "Damn, what happened now?"

She listened as the same report from the previous night aired and her heart rate monitor sped up as Brett's picture flashed on the screen. "Oh my God!" she placed her hand over her face and began to weep for him. She couldn't believe her eyes and ears.

"How can he be dead? Oh my God!" she said aloud. She was baffled and her feelings were tremendously hurt. She began wondering who was responsible. She thought back to the previous day when her father disappeared after she told him that Brett beat her and caused her injuries. "He couldn't be responsible," she said to herself. "Nah, he couldn't have done it," she dismissed the thought immediately-but not before grabbing the phone and dialing her house number.

The ringing of the phone startled Vernon while he lay in the bed looking up at the ceiling. He was still bothered by what had happened with Brett and hadn't been able the grasp the fact that a child had been murdered. However, he did what he felt he had to do to protect his child from another vicious attack. Another one could cost him his baby girl. That was a debt he wasn't willing to pay.

"Hello," he finally reached on the nightstand and picked up the cordless phone.

"Daddy!" CeCe wept into the phone.

"What's wrong baby girl?"

"Daddy somebody killed Brett last night, please tell me it wasn't you."

"Huh," Vernon answered. He was stalling while trying to gather his thoughts. "C'mon Baby Girl, you know better than that."

"I know Daddy, but what happened to him? I never wanted something like this to happen. Why is he dead?"

"How do you even know he's dead Pumpkin?"

"I just saw it on the news."

"Well what did they say?" he sat up as his heart started to race.

"They just said that he got killed and they didn't have any suspects."

"Well baby, don't let this upset you too much. Maybe he got what was coming to him. Maybe he beat on someone else. At this point, we don't know. So don't let that disturb you Sweet Pea. You just get better so I can come and get you. What did the doctor say?"

"He said if the tests come back fine they'll release me this morning. You coming to get me Daddy?"

"Of course I am; have I ever not been there for my Little Princess?"

"Nope," she answered with the sniffles. Her crying was soothed by her father's warm reassuring tone.

"So just get yourself together, and Daddy will be there shortly to see you?"

"Ok Daddy, I love you."

"I love you too Pumpkin."

As he placed the receiver down, he sat looking at himself in the mirror and contemplating his next move. He felt it was time for his baby girl to grow up. He had to let her know what really happened with Brett, and who he really was. Vernon knew this information would be a lot for young CeCe to digest, but he needed her full support from this point on. No more lies. "What have I done?" he asked himself. He was not as concerned with taking Brett's life as he was about CeCe's reaction when she learned the truth. No man should put his hands on a woman was his strong belief. The situation became personal when it was his daughter, and it had to be dealt with.

****

A knock at the door startled CeCe as she was flushing the toilet. She gathered up her IV and fixed her gown before exiting the bathroom to greet her visitor.

"Hey, you feeling better?" Chuck asked with a smile that made CeCe's eyes twinkle. She cracked a smile, but she was hurting inside about Brett's death.

"Hey you, yeah I'm feeling better. What you got in the bag?" she hungrily asked. Her stomach was grumbling at the site of food.

"Breakfast, as promised. We have steak, egg and cheese biscuits and Bo Rounds. I didn't know what you really liked to drink so I got you a Coke, is that cool?"

"Of course it is. It's the thought that counts. I'm about to starve!"

"Well, here you go." Chuck slid the tray over and put the food on it. He sat beside her, "Let's dig in. You need ketchup?"

"Yeah," she answered as they both began to devour the meals.

"Did you happen to catch the news this morning?" CeCe asked. She placed her hand over her mouth to try not to expose her food.

"Nah not this morning, but I saw the news last night. That dude Brett from The Hole got murdered."

"Yes! Oh my God, isn't that crazy?"

Chuck shrugged and continued to eat. He really didn't care about what happened to him. Somebody did his dirty work and beat him to the punch.

"Wow, you don't care?"

"Why would I care? I didn't even know him like that. Did you?"

CeCe knew she was treading dangerous waters and chose to pick her words carefully.

"Yes I knew him, and to me anybody losing their life is a sad situation. That could have been one of us. Sometimes we never take the time to be thankful for what we have and the lives we live every day. Murder is so wrong. What gives someone the right to take another's life?"

Chuck kept eating trying to ignore what she saying, but her beautiful innocent eyes gazing upon him made him answer. "Yeah, you're right, that was crazy. But sometimes people get what they deserve in life. How do we know that him and his friends didn't jump somebody, and they came back to get him? Karma is a bitch, and revenge is a dish best served cold."

CeCe found herself processing what he was saying to her. He was right. Brett was the reason that she had just lost a child and was damn near killed, although she could have done without the child part. Chuck's words made her begin to wonder if karma was the bitch that had her laying in the hospital bed now.

"Still, it's wrong. Two wrongs don't make a right," she finally spoke.

"Two wrongs don't make a right, but two rights don't make a left. Tomato, tamato; life happens you just have to deal with it."

"True!"

The two sat and ate and began focusing more on each other. She clung to his every word, as he was hung up on hers. He made her smile and she returned the favor. The two of them had no idea why they met, why they were having these feelings, or why they felt like they had known each other forever.

****

Carver High School

"Do you have any leads on that Wallace murder?" Officer Stokes asked Detective Brown as he was visiting the school trying to secure any leads on the case.

"Not yet. I have been up all night dealing with this case. I figured since he was a student here, I would come and find out what type of person he was," Detective Brown answered.

Detective Brown was a twenty-year veteran, with half of his time spent in the Homicide Unit. He had seen it all, and was the leading detective on the Wallace case. His dark complexion suggested that he was a frequent visitor to some tanning salon. He had a fuzzy brown mustache without a beard. The huge craters in his face gave him a Sicilian look, but he was originally from Texas. His body was lean and his pecks were developed from the many pushups that were included in his daily routine. He was one of the best at his craft, and for some reason he took this murder personally. He would never let his emotions show, but he was burning up inside. He was determined to find the answers to help him solve the case.

"Well yesterday he was involved in a fight with Chuck Jenkins, another student here."

The detective raised his right eyebrow and answered, "No shit," he then flipped open his pad and began taking notes.

"No shit. He and his friends jumped Mr. Jenkins yesterday. I don't know all of the boys that were with him, but I did recognize Eric Seals. He should be able to shed more light on the subject."

"I need to get these students down to the station and question them. Thank you for that information," Detective Brown offered his hand.

"No problem." Officer Stokes gave a firm grip. "Glad I could help."

****

Chuck gathered up all the trash from breakfast and tidied up a bit. The nurse came in and let them know that they were still waiting on the tests, but it wouldn't be long. They sat in the room and talked, lost in each other's words. A knock on the door startled them, "Hey Pumpkin," Vernon peeked in.

"Hey Daddy! Come in!"

Vernon walked inside and closed the door behind him. He usually was dressed casual, but today he was in a black Nike sweat suit, with a pair of Nike Air Raid shoes. He had on a black leather jacket and a toboggan to match. He still had the events of last night fresh on his mind, but he was not going to let it show.

"How you doing," Vernon extended his hand to Chuck with space for him to finally give up his name.

"Chuck," he answered shaking his hand.

Vernon walked around to hug and kiss CeCe.

"I see your friend is still here," he said to his daughter.

"Yes he is," she smiled.

"Well Chuck, I know you have been here a while, and I look forward to you coming by later for dinner so we can be formerly introduced. If you don't mind, I would like some time with my daughter. Can you be at our house by eight?"

"Eight sounds good to me sir," Chuck stood and said "I'll see you later CeCe."

"Ok," CeCe answered. "Make sure you're on time."

"I will," Chuck left the two of them and decided to go chill in the hood for a while with his boys.

"So how are you holding up Pumpkin?" Vernon began.

"I'm feeling better, I'm just ready to go home. I still can't believe what happened to Brett."

"Baby, I thought I told you to get that out of your head so you can get better."

"I know Daddy but I'm sad." Tears began to form in her eyes.

"That's my little girl, always the humanitarian. Baby, God doesn't make mistakes, and obviously it was his time to go. We can't question God and the decisions he makes."

Knowing her father was right; CeCe decided she would change the subject. "So, what do you think of my new friend?"

"What do you mean?"

"I mean, what do you think?"

"I think I'm going to hold my judgment until I get to know him a little better. I don't know anything about him. How much do you know about him?"

"I think he's sweet and I definitely haven't run into a nicer guy. Not many guys would have stuck beside me at a time like this; that says a lot to me."

"He seems fine, but don't be blinded by a smile baby girl. That guy Brett you were dealing with, how was he when you met him?"

Again, her dad was stinging her thoughts with the truth. Brett was the Alpha and Omega when they first met, and the way he slung that dick made him even dreamier. He had always been somewhat of an asshole, but every time he made her have an orgasm, she forgot about the negative qualities. It was his decision to start having sex without condoms, and he always told CeCe that he couldn't have kids so she had no need to worry. CeCe never thought of the other reasons that should have mandated their use.

Just as she was about to answer, the doctor strolled in.

"Hey, how are you feeling?" the doctor asked.

"I'm feeling better," CeCe replied.

"Good. Your tests came back clean, so the nurse will be bringing your things so you can change and get out of here. Do you guys have any questions for me?"

"Nope, just ready to get my baby home," Vernon said.

"Alright then, you'll have to sign the discharge papers and the nurse will brief you on her care."

****

Chuck was on the way to kick it in the hood, so he called Hakeem. He dropped out last year.

"Yo, what's the deal Blood?" Hakeem answered.

"Where you at bruh?"

"Man turn that damn radio down, I can't hear shit."

Chuck pressed mute on the radio remote control. "Can you hear me now? Anyway, where you at bruh?"

"Over here at Chelle and Nette crib, why you worried about it? Ain't you in school?"

"If I was at school, why would I have to turn the music down?"

"Yeah you right, my bad," Hakeem laughed and passed the blunt to Nette, "You coming through?"

"Yeah I'm coming, let me slide through the crib and pick something up then I'll be through. You got some smoke?"

"Yeah, I got you Blood. Scoop up some White Owls on your way."

"Bet," Chuck said as he ended the call.

Chuck pulled up in the small driveway and exited the vehicle to walk inside. He was going to grab some work before he went to catch up with Hakeem around the corner. He was clueless to the unmarked police car parked perpendicular to the house. As he got ready to leave the house, he spotted the officers through the living room window. He bolted toward the back door and was outside running as fast as he could.

"You go through the house, and I'll go around the side!" Detective Brown called out to his partner as he took off running around the building to catch his suspect.

Chuck gave it his all as he dashed through the projects with the cops on his tail yelling "Stop, Freeze!" He ran to the fence that surrounded the projects and climbed it like he was mixed with feline, but the black Polo sweat pants he was wearing snagged at the top of the fence. His body limply hung upside down as he squirmed back and forth trying to release himself. The two detectives scaled the fence as well and when they jumped over, Chuck was just falling to the ground. They drew their weapons and pointed them at his head.

"Don't fucking move!" Detective Brown hissed.

Chuck lay there with his arms stretched out submitting to the officer's request. His only thoughts were, "*Damn, at least I got rid of the dope.*" He was taken into custody and whisked away to the station to undergo questioning.

Hakeem watched the entire incident unfold from the front porch. He stood and wondered why the police were chasing his partner, hoping it wasn't because of the murder of T-Bone and Chico. "He bet not snitch on me," he thought as he puffed on the blunt and walked back inside. "Fuck that, I gotta deal wit' him."

Chapter 7

Chuck gazed upon the world from the back window of the police cruiser with a mood as gloomy as the smoke gray skies. The trees were bare, and the grass was covered with dead leaves that were once bright green. The sun was nowhere in sight, although it was approaching noon. The detectives pulled into the Public Safety Center; Chuck knew he was in for a long day. He was no stranger to this place; the last time he was here he was under investigation for a home invasion. He was cleared due to lack of evidence. The witnesses always seemed to change their stories once they received a visit from his local enforcer. The detective helped him out of the vehicle and ushered him inside.

Once inside, they boarded the elevator and headed to their destination. Chuck sighed and looked up at the camera watching him. The ride to the 5th floor wasn't long, and the detectives led him into Interrogation Room Three. They removed the handcuffs and left him alone.

"Man, this some bullshit." Chuck rubbed his wrists soothing the pain of the cuffs that were always placed too tight. He still didn't know why he was here, so he sat and waited for the first round of questioning.

The four officers stood watching Chuck and Eric on the tiny monitors that were hooked up to the interrogation rooms. Detective Brown, the lead on the case, was the first to speak.

"Eric told us this was the guy that he and Brett jumped at school yesterday because he was with Brett's girlfriend. Now we have to try to get a statement out of him so we can play these two back and forth against each other. What do we have on Chuck anyway?"

"We pulled his files, and he's been investigated for a home invasion that we couldn't get to stick. His name has been mentioned quite a few times downtown. He has seven cases the state has tried him on, and he's won all seven. His record is clean," Detective Santiago answered with his nose buried in the manila folder. Santiago was a nine year veteran on the force. He was originally from the Dominican Republic and had an accent to prove it.

"Oh yeah, he's going to be a tough nut to crack." Detective Simpson added. She was standing with her arms folded and ready for another chance to prove herself. She was the rookie of the bunch: sexy, sassy, chocolate, and very professional. She was one year removed from college, but she was quickly gaining a good reputation among her colleagues.

"I doubt it. You should join me Simpson and get some experience in cracking these tough nuts. They seem like they're not giving up any info, but they always do. They're gangster killers on the streets, but get em' in here," Detective Brown pointed at the monitor, "they start boo hooing and asking for tissues," he explained as they all shared a laugh.

Simpson tugged at her skirt, checked out her make-up in her compact mirror, and announced, "I'm ready, let's do this."

****

Chuck studied the officers as they entered the room; he grilled the white cop but could only smile when he saw the beauty of Detective Simpson. Her hair had a bounce like basketball in Magic Johnson's hands. Her wide hips swayed back and forth, and her breasts were jiggling like water balloons. Her chocolate skin and full lips enticed his dick to try to get a peek from under the table. They took a seat, and placed the folders on the table. Neither of the two spoke a word at first. They all sat studying each other. Chuck's eyes were cold and his emotions buried.

"I'm Detective Brown, and this is Detective Simpson. We would like to ask you a few questions."

"About what?" Chuck snapped.

"Where were you last night around 8 PM?" Brown asked him. He cut to the chase and got directly to business.

"What?" Chuck angrily retorted. "Man I was at the hospital wit' my girl last night."

"And what's this girlfriend's name?"

"Cynthia Harrison."

"Cynthia huh," Brown opened the folder and sat back. He threw his right foot across his left leg and leaned back. "Cynthia is *your* girl?"

"Ain't that what I just said?"

"Well according to Brett's friend Eric, Cynthia was Brett's girl."

Chuck's face quickly tightened up, "Why the fuck you bringing his name up? I saw on the news he got killed last night. I know ya'll ain't got me down here for that bullshit?"

"Did we say anything about you being down here for Brett? What makes you jump to that conclusion? You didn't kill him did you?"

"Fuck No!"

"Well you brought it up son, but go ahead and tell us about your relationship with Cynthia."

Chuck's mind and heart was racing. He thought he was down here for murdering T-Bone and Chico, but in fact he was being questioned about Brett. He had to make sure he treaded through his words carefully.

"Man it don't matter what our relationship is or isn't, I don't have shit to tell ya'll."

"Well let's try this," Detective Simpson parted her full lips and began to take over the questioning. "Tell us about the fight you had yesterday at school. What happened?"

Her beautiful hazel contacts made her eyes hypnotize Chuck as he spoke slowly, "I was with CeCe and we had just got back from lunch. I dropped her off at the back of the school and went to park my car. I walked past the dude Eric and his friends and ask em' why they were grilling me, then they jumped me. The guard at school broke it up and they took off running. I got up and went on about my business."

"CeCe is short for Cynthia, am I correct?"

"Yeah"

"So you dropped CeCe off, get jumped, and then what? How did she end up in the hospital? She was fine when you dropped her off."

"Well, we agreed to meet in front of the gym after school, so I was waiting for her after her class. While I was standing there, some chick ran upstairs screaming for help. I ran downstairs and saw CeCe laying on the floor. The ambulance took her away and I went to the hospital with her. I was there until like eleven. That's when I went home and saw on the news that dude got killed."

The detectives looked at each other and Brown finally said, "Okay, give us a minute." The two got up and left to go back to the monitors. They wanted to get the other detectives' opinion on what just transpired.

Chuck watched Simpson's fat ass make waves in that tight dress skirt. *"Damn I want some of that,"* he thought as he rubbed the erection that was starting to form. She was a sexy detective, but that didn't change the fact that she was there to send Chuck to prison on a 1ˢᵗ Degree murder charge.

"What do you guys think?" Detective Brown asked Santiago and Johnson who had watched the entire interview.

"It sounds like he could be telling the truth. We just have to get on the phone with the hospital to see if Cynthia was in fact there."

"I agree," Simpson took the lead, "We need to find her and talk to her as well. We need to know why she was in the hospital. It's ironic that he gets jumped when he dropped her off, and by the end of the day she's hauled off to the hospital. I feel like she knows something."

"Yeah, I think she definitely knows something. From the way Chuck was responding, it seemed that he knew nothing about her and Brett's relationship. He had it in his mind that she was his girl," Brown added.

If his story checks out, we can let these two go for now. Go ahead and release Eric, and keep Chuck for a little while longer until we can confirm if CeCe was in the hospital," Simpson concluded.

****

"Daddy, can we go by Forsyth Seafood so I can get something to eat? I'm starving," CeCe said as she turned to her father as they traveled down MLK and passed Winston Salem State University.

"Sure, I could use a good fish sandwich myself. I remember me, you and your mother used to eat there," Vernon said smiling while drifting off into a past memory. His wife had been dead for three years now but his heart never let her go. He hadn't forced himself to move on just yet.

"Yeah those were the days. Speaking of mom, when are you finally gon' meet a nice woman and start living again? Daddy I'm ready to see you happy; I can only do so much for you. It's time for you to move on."

Vernon looked over at his daughter and thought she was the spitting image of her mother. He knew she couldn't understand what he was going through. He really couldn't explain it to himself.

"Yeah, you're right baby girl. It is time for me to move on. I try. But I compare every woman I meet to your mother, and none of them can match her," he said as they pulled into the parking lot. "Come on, let's get some fish and we'll finish this conversation later. I have something else that we need to discuss too," Vernon said.

"Ok, but we're gon' talk about this Daddy. I'm worried about you."

The two went inside and headed straight over to the fresh fish section to view their options. They both agreed on the Red Snapper and ordered it fried with hush puppies, fries and cole slaw. They received their number and took a seat on the wooden bench to wait for their order. They chatted lightly until their number was called. Vernon went and picked up the order from the counter. On their way out CeCe resumed the conversation.

"So Daddy, you were telling me why you haven't found a nice lady yet," she flashed her pearly whites.

"Yeah, I'm just having a hard time moving on. I'm really trying Pumpkin."

"Try harder Daddy. You're a good man who deserves a good woman. I wouldn't mind having a step-mother one day. As long as you're happy, I'm happy. When you're sad, I'm sad Daddy," CeCe told him.

"That works both ways," he replied.

Vernon knew she was right. He knew that he needed to step out to cut a little rug and have some fun. He did have a jump off that he had sex with in the parking lot at work. But that was just sex; she wasn't worthy to meet his mother and daughter.

"You know what, I think I will go out tonight and have some fun. It's Friday and I have the night off. I think I'll have some fun as long as you're fine."

CeCe blurted out with excitement, "Yes! I'm good Daddy! I would love to help you pick out your outfit. Grandma will be goin' to Bingo tonight, so I'll make sure you're handsome."

"That sounds like a plan," he smiled and patted her on her thigh.

"What else did you want to talk to me about, Daddy? Vernon got caught up in the moment and forgot that he was planning to tell her what happened to Brett. He knew it would lead to many other questions and expose his hidden life. It seemed like a good idea in the room by himself last night, but he was second guessing that decision now.

"Ahh, I just wanted to talk to you about sex. Since I know you are having it now, I wanted to express the importance of using protection. CeCe there are lots of diseases out here. Condoms aren't only used for birth control."

"I know Daddy, and I have only had sex once without using one. We see how that turned out. I promise that I'll make sure I use them all the time from now on," CeCe lied.

"Good, you have to protect yourself these days. Better safe than sorry," Vernon replied.

****

"Ok Mr. Jenkins, you're free to go. You have a ride home?"

"I didn't drive here, did I?" Chuck snapped.

"Don't be a smart ass," Detective Brown spoke smugly.

"Look at my pants," Chuck pointed to the rip in his sweats.

"Nobody told you to run, now did they? You were running for a reason and we're damn sure gon' find out why. Let's go." Brown grabbed Chuck by the arm and led him to the elevator.

They walked back to same cruiser from earlier. "You can get in the front," Detective Brown said. "Tha fuck I look like? You must be crazy," Chuck responded while climbing in the back. His mind was racing while he gazed out the window. He couldn't figure out why Eric told the police his name, and why did they say Brett and CeCe were a couple. She told him she was single, and he had no reason to doubt her.

He didn't know who to trust right now. As they rode his mind went back to when he and CeCe pulled into the parking lot. He thought of how all of a sudden she wanted to get dropped off around back. He didn't think she saw the four man crew that jumped him. He only remembered her soft eyes locked on his.

"*CeCe wouldn't lie. Why wouldn't she? I don't even know this chick like that. She could be trifling like so many other bitches. Let me find out she trying to play me and this bitch is dead,*" Chuck thought as they pulled up in the projects. Detective Brown got out to open the back door and said, "Don't go too far. I got a feeling we'll be coming back to see you."

"Whatever," Chuck blew him off. He walked up the driveway to the door. As soon as the car pulled off, Hakeem came strolling from the path with his dreads sticking out from under the black hoodie. Chuck knew he was bout' to be on some bullshit, so he struck first.

"What up Blood?"

"You tell me, you the one getting chased by the police. Now they dropping you back off at home.

What's the deal with that shit woadie?" Hakeem's Louisiana accent kicked in.

"Come in man," Chuck motioned and the two went into the house. "Let me go change these pants and put some peroxide on this cut, I'll be right back."

Hakeem sat down in the living room with a cold menacing stare. The .44 on his hip had to be adjusted as he sat down. He decided it was too uncomfortable so he stood. He wasn't letting some rat bastard get him sent away for a murder, especially one that he didn't want to commit. He had come to murder Chuck.

****

"Daddy this was good." CeCe sat back in her chair rubbing her full belly.
"Yeah it was. So, are you still having company tonight?"
"Yeah, I guess. You invited him over, remember?"
"Yeah I remember, but that was before I decided to go out tonight. He's coming over around the same time I'm going out. I can't leave you in the house with a boy." Vernon gave her a look that screamed 'you must be crazy.'

"Why not Daddy? What can we possibly do? I was just released from the hospital, and I think I have had my share of the birds and the bees. I'm not going to be having sex for a long time," CeCe lied again.

How could she tell her father that her juice box was throbbing for Chuck's meat? The way it swung in his jogging pants earlier made her want to wrap her lips around it and see how much of it she could swallow.

She couldn't wait to ride his wood and grip her nails into his chest as she grinded on it. She could almost feel him poking around her insides while she made that pussy pop.

"Yeah, I hear you." Vernon answered. He didn't believe her at all. He just found out that she almost made him a grandfather before he was ready. He didn't want to talk about it anymore and switched the subject. "Well, I got the itis' after eating all that food; I'm gon' take a nap. Wake me up at six, if I'm already not up."

"If I'm even up myself, I got the itis' too. I didn't get much sleep last night. I think I'll get some rest and get up with you. I'll set the alarm clock, how 'bout that?" CeCe asked her father.

"Fine by me, get some rest Pumpkin and I'll see you later." He pulled his daughter close with one arm and kissed her forehead.

"Ok Daddy, love you."

"Love you too Pumpkin."

****

Chuck nursed the cut on his leg before throwing on another pair of sweats. After he got himself together, he started to walk out to talk to Hakeem. He was surprised to see him at his room door with his hoodie still on. He had both hands in the pouch.

"Damn Keem, you scared me. I was coming right out," Chuck said.

Hakeem tried to pull the .44 from the pouch. It was so long that he couldn't whip it right out, giving Chuck a chance to go for the gun. The two tussled in the hallway as the first explosion filled the air. The cannon's blast barely missed Chuck's leg.

"What the fuck you doing bruh?" Chuck yelled as they struggled. He never let go of the gun.

"I ain't going to jail for you woadie!" Hakeem screamed back. He was trying to aim the gun at Chuck's stomach.

"Boom! Another shot let loose as they continued to struggle. Chuck managed to turn the gun towards Hakeem's leg and forced his finger on the trigger. "Boom!" The third shot rang out.

The bullet ripped through Hakeem's leg causing him to scream, "Ahhh," but Chuck didn't let up. As he was falling backwards, Chuck fell with him and fired a fourth shot tearing through Hakeem's abdomen. Hakeem spewed blood in Chuck's face before he climbed off him with the gun in his hand. Chuck stood tall aiming the gun at Hakeem's head. He watched him balled up in the fetal position gripping his stomach.

"Man, what the fuck you thought? You thought you were gon' come and take me out? Dumb muthafucka."

Hakeem lay on the floor fighting for his life. He wanted to respond, but he couldn't. When he tried to speak, he coughed up blood. He looked up pitifully at Chuck standing over him. At that point he wished he could take it all back, or that he put a slug in the back of his head on the way in the house. It was too late for that now. He fought only a short time before his soul left his body and began its' journey into the afterlife.

Chuck watched as he squirmed and suffered and wanted to put a hole in his head. He knew better because he would be charged with first-degree murder. When Hakeem stopped struggling and submitted to the grim reaper, Chuck went and dialed 911. He knew he was on his way back to the interrogation room that he had left only an hour ago. He was ready for the manslaughter charge; he knew North Carolina didn't have a self-defense law.

Chapter 8

Chuck heard the sirens blaring in the background as the police and ambulance approached his house. His emotions were strained and his mind was racing. He was unsure if he should run, or wait for the police to arrive to take him to jail. He didn't want to run, so he decided to face the music.

The first car came to a screeching halt in front of his house. Chuck plopped down on the couch in the living room and waited. The officers knocked on the screen door, "Yeah, come on in," Chuck said. He looked at the white faces in the blue uniforms and gathered his thoughts.

"What happened in here?" The cop with the crew cut asked while holding his right hand on his holstered weapon.

"The body is in the hall," Chuck pointed where they needed to go.

"Go check it out," the officer instructed his partner, "What happened?" he repeated.

"I was coming out of my room, and my friend tried to shoot me. We fought over the gun and it went off in his hand and he shot himself."

"Ok, I'm going to need you to get up and place your hands behind your back. I'm going to have to take you into custody and take you down to the station."

Chuck sighed and reluctantly obliged with the request. The house began to fill with more police and emergency personnel. He was placed in handcuffs and led outside where nosy neighbors were all gathered. He was escorted out to the cruiser in the driveway, and shook his head as looked around the crowd for familiar faces. The officer placed Chuck in the back of the car and he waited to be hauled off for another interrogation.

****

CeCe heard the alarm blaring in her ears at 6:45 PM. Her room was dark; the sun had already set, and it made her feel like it was later than it actually was. She stretched and yawned trying to fight the urge to go back to sleep.

"Might as well catch the news to see if they caught anybody for Brett's murder," she said to herself as she fumbled around the bed looking for the remote. She flicked on the TV and started surfing the channels to see what was on.

She stopped when she reached the upcoming news stories and noticed the top story was another murder.

"Damn, these boys around here don't have anything better to do than kill each other," CeCe complained.

Winston-Salem had been having back to back murders since the crack epidemic devastated so many urban communities. It seemed as if everybody and their momma were selling or either using. The winters were mild, only totaling a few bodies-if that. However, the murders increased with the temperature. Spring and summer saw a steady annual increase. CeCe hated the fact that so many of her people were killing each other daily, but she was compelled to keep up with what was going on around her.

> "Tonight's Top Story: A Winston-Salem man has been murdered in the Sunshine Projects. Seventeen year old Hakeem Robinson went to a friend's house with intentions of murdering him, but in a battle over the gun he claimed his own life. Eighteen year old Chuck Jenkins was his intended target. Stay tuned for more details as they become available. No charges have been filed yet. The investigation is still under way. This marks the city's fifteenth homicide."

"What!" CeCe's eyes began to water as her heart was racing out of control, "Is this really happening?"

She reached for the phone and dialed Chuck's number. There was no answer. She tried his car phone, but was only prompted to leave a message at the beep. The tears rapidly began falling from her eyes, racing down her cheeks and dropping onto her shirt.

"I can't believe this is happening to me," she put her face in her hands and wept. She didn't know what to do, so she ran into her father's room, "Daddy, get up!" she yelled as she flicked on his light.

"Somebody tried to kill Chuck, but he killed them."

"What, who did what?" he sleepily asked.

"Chuck, Daddy, my new friend. Somebody went to his house and tried to kill him, but he killed the boy instead."

This news sat Vernon up, "When did this happen?" he asked. Before CeCe could answer, they heard a loud knock on the door that startled both of them. "Who is that Daddy?"

"I don't know," he got up and observed the undercover vehicle in the driveway. "It's the police."

His heart was pounding, but he couldn't show his daughter that the police's presence affected him. The gun that was used to murder Brett had been disposed of. After the vehicle pulled off from the murder scene, it was tossed in the same project neighborhood. Vernon felt that someone would pick the gun up and keep it. He was hoping that when they got caught with it, Brett's blood would be on their hands.

"What do they want Daddy?" CeCe hysterically asked.

"I don't know Baby, just stay here," Vernon instructed as he went to the door to address the situation.

****

Chuck nervously sat in the interrogation room chair with his chin resting on his fist. He was still trying to gather his thoughts and plot his best course of action. He had been at the station for about thirty minutes and had not been interviewed yet. As he impatiently sat and wondered when someone would come in, the door swung open and Detectives Brown and Simpson came strolling inside. They both sat down ready to begin the series of questioning.

"Ok," Brown spoke, "Tell us what happened in the house earlier."

Chuck's expression screamed anger, but he spoke rationally.

"Well, Hakeem saw ya'll drop me off earlier. As soon as the car pulled off, he came out of nowhere. He asked me what I was doing with ya'll, so I asked him to follow me inside while I changed my pants. When I came out the room," Chuck started acting out what happened, "He was trying to pull the gun out of his pouch. I grabbed it before he could get it out. We started fighting over it while he was pulling the trigger. He ended up catching two bullets."

The detectives listened and the story did match the evidence from the crime scene. Although there was no escaping the manslaughter charge, they were still looking for answers on Brett's case. They chose not to engage in any further conversation until their star witness arrived.

"Alright, we'll be back," Brown said as the two officers left the room.

****

"May I help you?" Vernon asked the two officers standing at the door.

"Yes, is Cynthia here?" the officer asked.

"Cynthia? Why are you looking for her? That's my daughter."

"Sir, we need her to come down to the station and answer some questions concerning a homicide."

"My daughter hasn't murdered anybody!" Vernon belted.

"We didn't say she did sir, but she has to come to the station and answer some questions. You're welcome to follow us to the station, but you can't be with her during questioning."

Vernon was processing the information he was being given when CeCe's voice called out from behind him, "Don't worry Daddy, I'll be alright."

He spun around and replied, "Ok Pumpkin, I'm going to be right behind you, let's go get our coats so we can go."

****

CeCe anxiously sat and looked around the room. She was concerned as to why she was here. What did the police want with her? Did they think she killed Brett, or had him killed? A million questions surfaced in her mind as the door opened, and Simpson and Brown entered the room. After taking a seat, Detective Simpson took the lead to attempt to connect with CeCe.

"How are you feeling today, Baby?" Simpson spoke, sounding like her mother used to when she wasn't feeling good.

"I'm fine, just kind of nervous that's all."

"Don't be, we just need to ask you some questions to clear up a situation. We have a dead kid who used to be your boyfriend, according to our sources."

"You mean Brett?" CeCe jumped into the specifics.

"Yes, Brett. Tell us about your relationship."

"Well, there isn't much to tell. We used to be together, but we broke up a while ago. We were still having sex sometimes," CeCe shrugged.

"Ok, so what's your relationship with Chuck?"

"I like Chuck, but we have only known each other for a few days. We just met, but he's sweet and caring."

"So did you ever give Chuck the impression that you were his girl, or that you were single when you met?" Brown inserted himself into the conversation.

CeCe studied his face and could tell that he was up to something and decided to choose her words carefully, "Like I said, we just met and I like him. Don't know what else I can tell you."

Simpson sensed the wall that CeCe was building and resumed the lead on the questioning. "Ok, you like Chuck. So what happened yesterday after school?"

"Well, I wasn't feeling good and I had to be rushed to the hospital. Chuck came with me, and was there until like eleven last night."

"And that's it?" Simpson asked in disbelief.

"Yep, that's it. What more do you want."

Simpson sighed and turned to Detective Brown, "You mind giving the two of us a minute?"

"Go right ahead," he slid his chair from the table and exited the room.

"Ok, so it's just me and you now. Let me let you in on some of the things that we know. We know you went out to eat with Chuck, and when ya'll returned to school you had him drop you off at the back of the building because you saw Brett. After you were dropped off, Brett and his friends jumped Chuck. We talked to the doctors and they confirmed that you indeed had a miscarriage from some blunt force trauma, and you had a hand print on your face," Simpson stated. She closely watched CeCe, and could tell she was breaking her down, so she continued. "So Brett and his friends jumped Chuck, and then he caught up with you after school and beat you too. You told Chuck who was responsible, and he went and murdered Brett."

"That's crazy lady! You don't know what the hell you're talking about! Chuck was with me at the hospital and couldn't have killed Brett. Ask the nurse, she can confirm he was there. The doctors don't know shit," CeCe said angrily as the tears flowed.

"Ok, so you're saying Brett wasn't the one who beat you?"

"No, what? Wait a minute," CeCe was confused. She didn't know what was going on, but she knew she didn't like it.

"You better start coming clean before you're charged as an accessory to murder."

"I didn't do anything!" CeCe screamed at the top of her lungs, but Simpson didn't even blink an eye.

"So I guess if we tested Brett and the dead fetus-it wouldn't be his huh."

"Ok!" CeCe broke down, "Yes he was the father, and yes he was the one who beat me. I admit it. But I swear, Chuck was at the hospital with me and couldn't have killed him. You have to believe me."

"Now why should I believe you? You had a chance to come clean, but you gon' try to play us like we don't know shit," Simpson let out a short laugh. "You must think we're stupid."

"I promise that's it, nothing more than what I told you. Chuck did not kill Brett, just check with the hospital!"

"Ok CeCe, I'll check. If I find out you're lying, I'll be back to charge your ass with accessory after the fact to a homicide," Simpson told her. She then left to go speak with her team, who sat watching the entire exchange.

CeCe folded her arms on the desk, buried her face in her sleeves, and wept like a baby. She knew Chuck couldn't have killed Brett; he didn't even know that Brett was the one who beat her. She was getting that lonely feeling again and a feeling of emptiness started to surround her.

"So, what do you guys think?" Simpson asked the other detectives on the case.

"I think she's telling the truth, but something just isn't adding up. If Chuck was at the hospital at the time of the murder, then who killed Brett?" Detective Brown asked.

"Yeah you're right, who could have done it?" Simpson took a seat, tapping the pen on the desk.

"Have we looked into her father? I mean he would have motive," Brown pointed out.

"Yeah he would, but how do we tie him to the murder? What evidence do we have so far?"

"We don't know if we have the gun yet, but a .357 Magnum was turned in. We're waiting for the ballistics report. I was going to use that to scare Chuck, but it looks like we would have been barking up the wrong tree. We also have tire tracks on the street; if we could match the tire treads to the father's car, then we may have something. The ballistics results should arrive in about two weeks, so I say we let her go and book Chuck on Manslaughter. He has a considerable amount of money on him, so he'll most likely make bond. We have lots of work to do."

****

Chuck was booked, but made the $15,000 bail. CeCe sat with her father waiting for the bondsman to finish up the paperwork. Meanwhile, police officers were outside taking pictures of the tire treads on his car.

It took almost forty-five minutes before Chuck came strolling from the back. CeCe ran into his arms and he squeezed her tightly. The hug made them both feel secure with one another and their hearts seemed to beat to the same drum. It was as if they belonged together. No other female ever fit between his arms so perfectly.

Vernon sat back watching with a blank stare on his face. His mind drifted off to his first meeting with his wife and their first hug. Not wanting to get too emotional, he looked away. CeCe had to practically peel herself away from Chuck.

"Let's get out of here," CeCe said, and Chuck draped his arm around her as the three of them left the building.

The ride home was eerily quiet. Finally Vernon asked, "You alright back there?" while looking over his shoulder at Chuck.

"Yeah, I'm cool. I'm just tripping off the day's events. I haven't even talked to my mom, and I know she's mad about the house. I don't even know if I can go back home right now. My best friend just died in my house. Hakeem was my boy," Chuck started, but got choked up as the tears fell from his eyes.

"You can come to our house for the night. You were there for my daughter and we'll be there for you. I can imagine how you feel about your friend. I have lost someone close to me too."

"Did you kill them?"

"No, cancer did but I couldn't save her. It was my wife, CeCe's mother."

"Oh, sorry to hear that."

"No, it's fine" CeCe cut in. "My mom is in a better place and she wants us to be happy while she's looking over us."

"Well, watching my boy die was crazy to me. He actually tried to kill me. I feel like I can't trust nobody in my hood no more. I'm gon' have to move. I can't live in that house; it's time for me to get out on my own. My mom doesn't have time for me anyway. It's time to be a man," Chuck said.

"You haven't even graduated from high school yet. Don't grow up too fast, but I understand where you're coming from. Just give it some time," Vernon told him as they pulled into the driveway.

They exited the car and walked inside. Vernon went and took a shower to get ready to put in some work tonight. His mother was supposed to be home around the time that he would be leaving. He wasn't really worried about CeCe and Chuck doing anything since she was still fresh out of the hospital, and Chuck had a horrible day.

Little did he know, but CeCe's love box was working just fine. She had been waiting for a night with Chuck. All she could think about was wrapping her lips around his stick to see where she could drive him. Crazy was the destination, and all the porno's she had been sneaking to watch with Brett had her skills up to par.

Chuck's mind was still cluttered and trying to process the events of the day. All he could think about was Hakeem stretched out on his floor, dead. Hakeem wasn't the first person he murdered, but he was the first person he committed a murder with. Now he was gone, and his blood was literally on Chuck's hands and clothes.

Chapter 9

"Well CeCe, I thought your grandmother would be here by now. I guess she stayed late at Bingo, so I'll see ya'll in the morning. You two ok?" Vernon asked as he slid on his coat and grabbed his keys from the key rack.

"Yeah Daddy, you be careful."

"I will, and Chuck keep your head up. I don't mean the one in your pants. I see you're hurting, but it's going to be alright."

"Daddy!" CeCe said, embarrassed by the joke.

Chuck let out a slight laugh at Vernon's remark and responded, "Thanks sir, CeCe's safe with me. Don't worry."

"Aight, ya'll be good. I gotta get out of here," Vernon told them as he walked out, shutting the door behind him.

CeCe listened for his car to leave before she turned to look at Chuck. She had never really concentrated on his looks, until tonight. He could use a haircut, but his skin looked soft and smooth. He had no signs of acne, which told CeCe that he took good care of his skin. He didn't have much facial hair, but his mustache was getting fuller by the day. His lips curved nicely and were just the right shade of pink. Luckily, all the weed smoking had not turned them black yet. His eyebrows were full and his lashes were long and pretty, almost like a female's. However, there was nothing else feminine about him. Chuck was all man, and CeCe couldn't wait to sink her teeth into him.

"What are you thinking about?" she asked as she sat on the couch next to him. She pulled one of her legs from underneath her and propped her elbow up on the back of the couch. She sat there staring at him.

"I don't know," he shrugged, "I guess I'm still tripping off the fact that Keem was my boy and he tried to kill me. I don't know if I can trust anyone now."

CeCe didn't really care if Chuck had friends; she wanted to feel his dick in her mouth and throbbing pussy right now. "Well I see you looking tense," she said while twirling her hair and giving him her sexy look, "Let's go up to my room and get comfortable. I can give you a massage."

Chuck was still upset about Hakeem, but the invite made him forgot about those feelings. "Yeah, we can definitely do that. First, I wanna get this blood off me," he reminded her.

"Come on; let me get you in this hot shower. Give me your clothes so I can wash 'em. My grandma won't be here for another two hours or so."

"Aight," Chuck stood up and peeled his shirt off. CeCe's panties were immediately soaked.

His abs were like a step ladder for her eyes as she climbed each one by one. His chest was nicely cut and his nipples poked out a little. When he pulled his jogging pants down, his boxers went down a little. It exposed a bush and his pelvic muscles. CeCe thought he looked like one of the guys from a magazine. She already knew he was packing, so she wasn't surprised by the way his inches slung left to right. *"I can't wait to get that in between my lips,"* she thought. She licked her lips and admired his muscular legs. All the time spent playing basketball really had Chuck in shape.

"Ok, let me get these in the wash machine. Go to my bathroom upstairs," she pointed. "Make a left and it's the second door on the right."

CeCe walked off to get his clothes started, as Chuck made his way upstairs. He flicked on the light and noticed how neat and clean her bathroom was. It was very spacious; the color scheme was a cream and burgundy with a flower border lapping around the wall at the top. The bathtub was sparkling white and matched the toilet and sink. He knew she was clean.

CeCe placed the clothes in the machine and headed upstairs. She made a pit stop at the hall closet to get a towel and washcloth, then sashayed her ass into the bathroom. Chuck was bent over the tub checking the water's temperature with his hand; she kicked him playfully in the butt.

"Hey!" he turned around laughing, and scooped her in his arms like he was going to slam her.

They both broke out into giggles and felt a closeness that neither of them had experienced in their young lives. Her body felt so soft under his. When he looked down into her eyes both of them had passionate expressions. Her 5'2" frame hung under his 5'10" body like a Van Gogh picture on a wall.

"This just feels so right," CeCe spoke softly.

Chuck began to lower his head and his eyes closed as their lips locked onto each other's for a brief kiss. That wasn't enough to satisfy the hunger the two felt for each other, and they engaged in a serious tongue wrestling match. The kiss was heavenly as their heads twisted and turned. His hands firmly gripped her ass causing his fingers to sink deeper.

She rubbed his head and before she knew it her shirt began to rise. She pulled away to help him out, and out popped her perky titties sitting nicely in her red lace bra. Their lips locked again as if they were magnets. The kiss was so passionate that CeCe started tugging at her own shorts.

"Let's get in the shower," she suggested as the steam from the shower was already creeping through the air.

She watched him as he removed his boxers and was impressed by his package. She couldn't wait to try something new with her new boo. He turned to peel the curtain back, and she wanted to bite his buns. They were shaped so perfectly.

Chuck stepped in the tub. The hot water was stinging at first, but watching CeCe remove her panties took his mind away from it. Her body was soft and curvaceous. The way her hips swayed with every step she took made his dick rise an inch.

CeCe stepped inside and was hiding behind Chuck. She used his body as a shield from the water. He turned to face her. Her heart was fluttering while her juices were flowing beneath. She went in for another kiss, enjoying him even more than the first time. They felt like they belonged together.

Chuck's hands began exploring her body; he stopped and gripped her supple booty. Their bodies were skin to skin, and he never experienced feelings so strong for a girl. He had envisioned this moment since she smiled at him in front of the gym on the day they met.

CeCe finally broke free from his lips and began lathering up the washcloth. She proceeded to wash every inch of him as he ran his washcloth across her body as well. She didn't waste time using the rag once she grabbed a hold of his nice, long, hard dick. Chuck's hand was playing with her clit and it was driving her crazy, so she decided to drop to her knees and put the wood in her mouth.

Chuck watched as she went down, and yelled "Ohhh shit," as she inserted his manhood into her mouth. She worked her hands back and forth. She was twisting and turning her head and wrists driving him crazy. He felt so good in her mouth. His moaning sounds let her know that the pornos were paying off. She continued to work her hands and her mouth in unison as water dripped from over his shoulders down on her head. Usually CeCe would not fathom getting her hair wet, but not now-not tonight.

She was driving Chuck crazy. Her mouth felt like a warm oven. He had never received head like this before, and he couldn't control himself. He tried to hold it back, he tried to think about basketball, but it didn't work. "Oooooo shhhhhh," he yelled out, as the nut came bursting from the head of his dick and into CeCe's mouth.

CeCe immediately pulled away and spit the wad of semen in the bottom of the tub. She looked up, "Damnit Chuck! Why didn't you tell me you were about to cum?" she spat. She angrily got off the floor of the tub and stepped out onto the bathroom floor.

"Damn Baby, my bad. I was trying to tell you," Chuck said.

"Trying to tell me," she cut him off, "I didn't hear you say you were cumming, not one time," she continued spitting. She was obviously disgusted with the situation.

"I'm sorry," he reached out to try and hug her, but she pushed him away.

"Get the fuck off me Chuck! I can't believe you just did that shit," she yelled. She stepped out of the shower, grabbed her towel and stormed out of the bathroom, slamming the door behind her.

"*Damn,*" Chuck said to himself as he continued to let the water run over him. He never anticipated that she would act like this about it. "*Oh well,*" he got over it quickly and began to finish bathing as his erection started to decline. "*At least I bust a nut,*" he thought while he finished bathing.

CeCe stormed into her room pissed. She was talking to herself, "I can't believe that muthafucka came in my mouth, I'm not sucking his dick no more."

She kept playing out what he had done, but then began to ask her self, "*Was it really that bad?*" Brett never came in her mouth, but she had never put her mouth on him like she did Chuck. Her anger went from a five, back down to a level one, eventually disappearing altogether. "*I gotta feel that thing inside me,*" she thought. Chuck stepped inside with water still glistening on his body.

"I'm sorry Baby," he said softly and took her into his arms.

They began to kiss on one another. His dick jumped back up and her juices began to flow. It was like nothing had ever happened. They were both so engulfed in each other that they wouldn't have heard the front door. Luckily for them, Vernon had a security system installed the day after CeCe was caught in the house with Brett; they heard the chime when the door opened.

"Oh shit!   That's my grandma, go back to the bathroom," she whispered. Chuck took off headed back in that direction.

She hustled to throw on some clothes and then ran downstairs to speak to her grandmother and put Chuck's clothes in the dryer.

"Hey Grandma!" she joyfully said as she breezed past her. Ms. White was looking through the mail on the counter in the kitchen.

"Hey child," she answered back smugly.

"Did Daddy call you?"

"Yes, he called and told me you had male company. I had to cut my evening short, the two of you better not been in here doing anything. Where is he?"

"He's in the shower," CeCe answered. She took his clothes from the washing machine and placed them in the dryer.

"I had to wash his clothes because they were covered in blood."

"Covered in blood? My Lord, what happened to him? Why was he covered in blood?"

Her grandmother gave her a condescending look. Ethel didn't play no games. She had raised Vernon, as well as four other children. The others were all off living their own lives and raising their children. Vernon was always her favorite child, and for some reason he didn't want to leave his mother like everyone else. Ethel was short; maybe 5'3" and she was as round as a pumpkin. Her arthritis in her knee caused her to walk with a cane when she went out in public, but she was fine waddling around the house. She was the epitome of a strong black woman, but her cute caramel face and light grey hair hid the fact that she had been through many trials and tribulations in her life.

"His friend tried to kill him and they fought over the gun; he ended up killing his friend."

"Oh my Lord," she covered her mouth with her hand, "that's awful, is he ok?"

"Yeah that fucker is ok, he came in my mouth," CeCe thought. "Yeah, I think he is. He hasn't really said much since he got here," she answered.

"Well baby, you have to approach that situation with caution. Losing a friend is hard, killing a friend has to be even harder. I wonder if he wants anything to eat?"

"I don't know," CeCe shrugged, "I don't think he does. He's in the shower right now, and when his clothes dry I'm sure he gon' probably go to sleep."

"Well I'm tired, so I'm going to bed. I'll fix you both some breakfast in the morning."

"Thanks Grandma, I love you."

"I love you too baby."

****

Chuck sat in the bathroom with his heart pounding in his chest. A soft knock on the door snapped him out of his zone, "yes," he answered politely not sure who was on the other side.

"It's me, open up."

He draped the towel around his waist and opened the door to see CeCe with a huge smile on her face. "What you smiling for?" Chuck asked.

"What, I can't smile now?"

"Yeah you can. What did your grandmother say?" he asked with a hint of worry across his face.

"She didn't say anything. Her room is downstairs, so she just went to bed because she was tired."

"That's it?"

"What else would she say? It's not like you were digging me out, making me scream O Chuck!" CeCe said laughing.

"Shhhh," he put his finger to his mouth, "You tripping."

"Boy stop actin' crazy, she can't hear shit downstairs. She's going to bed. You can go lay down in the guest bedroom. I'll bring your clothes when they're finished drying."

"Where is it?"

"The room right next to mine with the door closed. The one at the other end of the hall is my father's."

"He gotta sleep close to you to make sure don't nobody dig in that kitty kat." Chuck said and started laughing.

"Shut up," she hit him playfully, "Go 'head, and I'll be in there in a few."

"Aight."

Chuck laid down and didn't realize how tired he was, and how the events from the past few days had taken a toll on him. The T-Bone and Chico murder kept playing out in his head, as well as Hakeem taking his last breaths in the hall of his house. It was too much death and too much crazy shit happening around him. It made him terribly drowsy, and he dozed off into a deep sleep in minutes.

CeCe peeked inside and noticed Chuck was asleep so she closed the door behind her. She laid the clothes she had in her hand on the dresser, and then stepped over to the bed. One by one she removed the articles of clothing she wore. She slid the towel from over his dick and stuck it back in her mouth. She was over the fact that he came in her mouth.

He opened his eyes slowly and began to moan, he rubbed the back of her head. She was doing her thing. She was bobbing and weaving like Sugar Ray Leonard, his dick was standing straight up by the time he came to. She didn't waste any more time. She jumped up and hopped on his dick.

At first he thought, *"Damn, I'm not even wearing a rubber."* When he felt her warm, tight walls grab a hold of his meat; he gripped her ass and helped her bounce up and down. *"Damn this some good pussy,"* he thought.

"Ohh shit Daddy, this dick is good," she called down to him as her claws were dug into his chest. She bounced up and down on him as his dick made its way to her stomach.

"Ugh, Ugh, Ugh," she said as each stroke brought her closer and closer to her climax. *"Damn this dick is good,"* she said to herself as she continued to moan. CeCe jumped up and down on the dick like she was riding a raging bull. She made the bed springs bounce with her; Chuck was tearing that ass up.

"Fuck," he said as he gripped her ass and slid his middle finger into her asshole. "Oh shit," CeCe said, "I like that." Her pussy got wetter and wetter, and Chuck knew he was nearing his climax, "*Oh shit, what I'm gon' do this time,*" he tried to ask himself. Once again, it was too late. He emptied his load inside of her.

Her juices were flowing out of control, and his dick kept hitting that spot. CeCe dug her nails deeper into his chest until finally she threw her head back and exploded all over him. She didn't even notice that he came right before she did. She really wasn't thinking about it. The dick was good, and it had her mind gone. She rode it until she couldn't stand it anymore, and fell down on top of him with her body shaking uncontrollably. Never had she felt a feeling quite like this, and she held onto him for dear life.

As she crashed on top of him, Chuck wrapped his arms around her. This was hands down the best pussy that he had ever run up in. They lay on the bed and held each other. CeCe hopped up after a few minutes.

"I have to go to the bathroom to wipe myself off and go get in the bed. Sorry I couldn't make you cum and I came too soon."

"It's cool, I got mine earlier remember," he lied.

"How can I forget," she leaned back in to kiss him, "I'll see you in the morning. You can go in the bathroom when I'm done," she told him. She gathered up her clothes, and left.

"Damn," he put his hands behind his head and gazed at the dark ceiling, I think I love her."

Chapter 10

The familiar smell of bacon frying on the stove drifted upstairs and filled Chuck's nostrils. He awoke from a restful night's sleep with CeCe still on his mind. She really did her thing last night, and he handled her like a real man should have. The scratches on his chest provided visible proof that he took care of business.

He grabbed his clothes from the dresser; they had the fresh smell of Gain laundry detergent and Snuggle fabric softener. He removed the towel from his waist and noticed his morning wood was at full attention. He proceeded to get dressed and went into the bathroom seeking relief. On his way to the bathroom, he noticed that CeCe was already up.

"Hey you," he lightly said while standing in the door way watching her brush her hair in the mirror.

"Hey," she stopped stroking her hair for a moment and turned around to greet him.

"Put that thing away," she said pointing to the bulge in his pants.

"You didn't say that last night," Chuck laughed.

CeCe cracked a sly smile, "I sure didn't, did I," she replied.

"Something smells good downstairs, who cooked?"

"My grandma's fixing breakfast and my dad should be here soon so we can eat. Go 'head and wash yourself up and we'll go downstairs so you can meet her."

"Aight," he answered as he retreated to the bathroom to pee and wash his face. Since he didn't have a toothbrush, he used a wash cloth to brush his teeth. Chuck was from the projects, this wasn't the first time he had done this. He knew how to adapt to any situation.

After he finished in the bathroom, he joined CeCe and walked downstairs to finally meet her grandmother. His stomach felt like he needed to run back upstairs and take a good shit, but it was only butterflies and nervous energy. Chuck took a deep breath, and walked in behind CeCe.

"Hey Grandma!" CeCe said then turned to point, "This is my new friend Chuck."

"Good morning, how you doing?" Chuck asked nervously as she looked him up and down with a smirk.

"Smells good Grandma, what we having?"

"Chile, you sitting her looking at the pots, can't you see what we having."

"*Oooo,*" CeCe thought, but she sighed and replied, "I love you too." Her grandmother was always flipping the script. One day she was the nicest, sweetest lady you could ever be around. The next day she would be an evil bitch. If it wasn't for her father, she and her grandmother wouldn't be able to live under the same roof.

She motioned for Chuck to join her at the kitchen table when she heard her father's keys jingling and fumbling its way into the hole. Vernon stepped in with a million dollar smile; he looked like he had just had great sex. He did hit his usual piece at work, but that wasn't the reason for the smile.

"Hey Daddy!" CeCe called out.

"Hey Baby Girl, good morning," he leaned in to kiss his daughter on the forehead. He then turned to Chuck, "How are you feeling this morning?"

"I'm feeling better sir, thank you." Chuck nervously responded. He was wondering if Vernon could tell that he had dug in CeCe's guts last night.

"Good," he turned back to his daughter, "Let's go do some shopping today. Remember that check that I lost?"

"Yeah, I remember," CeCe's eyes lit up.

"Well," he reached in his shirt pocket, "They gave it to me at work last night."

"Yes!" CeCe jumped up and grabbed his neck and hung on tightly.

Chuck watched the bond that Vernon shared with his daughter. He didn't have a relationship like that with anybody, and his heart had turned cold. He never really had anything or anybody who loved him except Hakeem, and look how that turned out. He was really a loner now and he knew it was time to leave the projects. He knew his mom wasn't worried about him, but he wanted to go home and see her. Not only did he have to face her, but he had to face the projects. The evil stares, the gossip, and the rest of the crew. *"I wonder if I should kill them all?"* Chuck asked himself.

"So Chuck, what time did you want to go home," Vernon asked. He took his usual place at the head of the wooden table.

"After breakfast, if that works for you. I have to get my car and catch my mom before she goes back to sleep. She usually gets up early and I have to be ready for this lecture."

"That'll be fine."

Grandma started placing the food down at the center of the table. As the southern tradition dictated, everybody made their own plates. They passed the dishes around the table so everyone could help themselves. The smell of bacon, eggs, grits, toast and potatoes and onions filled the air. She took her seat at the other end of the table and CeCe and Chuck sat at both sides. She stretched her hands out towards the kids.

"Come on, let's bow our heads in prayer," she said as they all gripped hands and bowed their heads. "Lord, bless this food we are about to receive, and let it nurture and replenish our bodies, Amen."

"Amen," everybody said in unison, before dropping their hands and grabbing plates. They barely conversed as the plates went around. The food smelled delicious and they started digging in immediately. Chuck was really feeling this breakfast with family. He had hopes of having his own family one day, maybe with CeCe. He couldn't live with his mom in the projects anymore; he wanted bigger and better things for himself and his new girl. It was time to set his plan in motion.

CeCe felt like this breakfast wasn't her grandmother's best. She quickly ate her food and almost rushed everyone else. She was ready to go get rid of Chuck and go shopping. She liked Chuck, and the sex was great, but as usual she started to lose interest after she had sex with him. CeCe was, in many ways, like a man when it came to sex. After she got what she wanted, she was on to the next one.

Vernon and CeCe got ready for a day at Hanes Mall. Chuck sat in the living room waiting to go home and trying to figure out what he was going to say to his mother. He had no idea what to say, but he was gon' make up something. *"Why I can't tell her the truth?"*

he asked himself, but the answer came back, *"Cause she never believe shit I say."*

The three pulled out and headed to the Sunshine Projects. Chuck gazed at the scenery as the trees and houses flew by. CeCe and her dad were engaged in conversation, but Chuck tuned them out. When they turned into the projects, his eyes scanned from porch to porch looking for Tony and Harold.

"Pull over right there," Chuck pointed to where his car sat.

"Ok, you be easy. I know it's going to be hard going back in the house where you killed your friend, but try not to think about it too much," Vernon assured him.

"Aight thanks sir, I appreciate everything. I'll call you later CeCe."

"Ok Chuck," CeCe answered quickly so he could get out and go. The mall was calling her name.

****

"They're stopping here in the Sunshine Projects dropping off Mr. Jenkins," Officer Martinez called in on the radio after following the trio from the house.

"So you think they all had something to do with it?" his partner, Officer Hannon, asked with a southern drawl. Hannon was a married man from Conway, South Carolina. He was the smallest detective on the force standing at 5'2" and weighing only 115 pounds. He had a bald head and a light brown complexion. "It looks like they all working together. They bailed the kid out of jail and let him spend the night at their home.

They all have to be in on it, but I wonder who pulled the trigger?" Martinez questioned as he took off and kept following the mark, leaving Chuck to go about his business.

****

Chuck gathered his thoughts and worked up the nerve to walk into the house. He noticed everybody watching him, and had a good idea of what they were saying about him-but he didn't give a fuck. This wasn't the first time he killed, and it didn't matter to him if he had to do it again. There was no sign of Tony and Harold, but he knew they were somewhere watching.

He snatched open the badly chipped white wooden screen door with the wire mesh window. He heard the TV on, inserted the key into the hole, and entered the house. It was junky as usual, but the crime scene made it extremely worse.

"Ma!" Chuck called out, but he didn't hear an answer.

He walked through the house and looked in his mother's room and noticed she was sleeping. He knew he wanted to get this conversation over with, so he went in to wake her.

"Ma," he said while shaking his mother. She didn't budge. "Ma," he shook her again, but she still didn't move.

He stuck his finger under her nostrils and noticed that she wasn't breathing. He started getting nervous and was on the verge of panic. "Ma! Get up Ma!" he called out trying to lay her on her back to administer

CPR. Although he was not trained to give it, he tried doing what he saw people do on TV. Tears furiously fell from his eyes, his heart fell into his stomach, and he felt like he couldn't breathe. He ran for the cordless phone and hysterically called 911. He cursed and yelled into the phone so much that the dispatcher could barely understand a word he was saying. The 911 operator was able to trace the call and send help his way. Unfortunately, nothing he could do would help his mother at this point; she was already resting in peace.

****

"Here's two hundred dollars to go shop with," Vernon said as he reached in his pocket to grab the money, "I have to run up the street and take care of something, and I'll be right back," he told CeCe as they pulled up to the mall.

"Daddy," CeCe whined giving him the puppy dog eyes that made him melt, "I wanted you to come with me," knowing she couldn't wait for him to pull off. She loved her dad, but this was Hanes Mall on a Saturday. Everybody was gon' be out here, and she was looking good. She wore her black stretch pants and a big T-shirt that hung off the shoulder, exposing the black tank top she had on underneath. Her hair was in a fresh mushroom do, and her Reebok Classics with the black and white shoe laces set her outfit off. The 'CeCe' that was airbrushed on her shirt matched her bamboo earrings which read the same.

"Baby Girl I'll be right back, don't trip."

"Don't trip?" she leaned up against the window giving her father a face that screamed 'really,' "Who you been around that got you trying to be hip? Let me find out you got a boo you not telling me about Daddy."

"What?" he laughed at his daughter's silly look. "I'm hip, what you mean? Your father ain't old and washed up, I still got it you know," he replied.

He was really on his way to have sex with his friend from work; she lived down the street from the mall.

"Whatever," CeCe laughed, then hugged and kissed her father on the cheek, "Love you Daddy!"

"I love you too Pumpkin," he embraced his daughter.

"Ok, so can you just come and get me when I page you?"

"Yeah just beep me when you're done, and don't be out here being all fast either," he gave her that 'you know better' look.

"Bye Daddy," CeCe stepped out closing the door behind her. She turned to the mall and was excited to see all the traffic; she was ready to see and be seen.

****

Chuck couldn't believe everything that was happening to him. First, Hakeem and now his mother-nothing made sense to him anymore. He listened to the police cars racing to his residence once again. They were coming to tag and bag another body. This time, it was the last person he had left in the world. His mom was about to be bagged up and shipped to the morgue. He sat with tears streaming hard at first, but they stopped flowing all of a sudden. He made his mind up, he was done crying, he was done feeling sorry, he was about to stand on his own two feet and man up. He was contemplating his next move. He could not stay this house another night. There was too much pain that consumed these walls.

The police and ambulance arrived. The officers and rescue workers came inside and did their jobs in his mother's room. Chuck sat and waited for the drama to end. He sat on the edge of the bed and stared into the hall. It was like his mind was playing tricks on him. He kept seeing Hakeem looking up at him with blood spewing out of his mouth. He had to close his eyes and shake that image from his head. He reopened them to see an officer letting him know that they were finished and leaving.

He got up to watch his mother being rolled outside, and placed in the ambulance. There were no flashing lights, and it pulled off so peacefully. As the police and rescue workers left, he saw two faces that he didn't really want to see come bopping across the street. It was Tony and Harold.

****

CeCe pranced around the mall, looking for her two favorite people in the world her girls Destiny and Erica. They all attended different schools, but had been friends since they used to attend the Boys and Girls Club together. They didn't get to hang out as much as they used to, but when they did the times were epic!

Destiny had the bubbly personality that kept everybody laughing. She was constantly cracking jokes. She was also a classic hood chick; she didn't care about anybody's feelings, she said whatever came to mind. She was like a feisty little Chihuahua, 5'3" and 98 pounds on a fat day. She had a caramel complexion and long coarse hair that she usually wore permed. Destiny was the thug of the crew, but none of them could ever be mistaken as hood girls. They all grew up in the suburbs and had never experienced being poor.

Erica was the white girl of the crew and she loved black culture. Her parents were the coolest, and racism didn't exist in her home. She had always hung out and played with all the black kids in her middle class neighborhood. Erica's skin was a beautiful creamy white, and her body had a better shape than most of the black girls her age. She had a booty that jiggled when she walked, and breasts that waved 'heyyyyy' to all the boys when she sashayed past. She had more of a voluptuous build with thick hips and thighs, but her stomach was flat. She looked like she ate plenty of grits, cornbread, and other foods that stuck to her southern bones. Her hair was blonde and usually cut into a short bob. She hated her hair, but used it to accent her natural money green eyes.

"Come on ya'll, let's go to the other side of the mall and hit up The Cookie Factory. I want some of them chocolate chip cookies," CeCe suggested.

"Girl, do I look like I need to eat anybody's chocolate chip cookies?" Erica said waving her hands at her body to showcase.

"Girl bye, you know you PHAT," Destiny chimed in.

"Pretty, Hot, and Tempting is what you are girl, so stop tripping and let's go," CeCe joked and they began their journey.

The three were definitely turning heads and had a pack of wolves following them like they were prey. As their asses twisted, turned and bounced Jay Jay, Troy and Kevin were mesmerized. The mall was packed with young ladies, but none matched this clique. The fellas were determined to meet them and were about to get their chance.

"Let us get the three cookies for a dollar," CeCe told the cashier and turned to her friends, "Ya'll want some milk with that?"

"Ewww, no!" Destiny answered. Erica cut in, "Yeah, I want milk with mine. Milk does the body good, you should drink more of it," she teased Destiny referring to her skinny frame.

"Whatever, get me a Coke," Destiny blew off the snide remark.

"Yeah, get us something too," a deep voice tapped on the ladies' eardrums.

The girls spun around to see whose mouth that voice came from and were pleased with the smiles on the three young men's faces. Jay Jay was the vocal one, chocolate, tall, and baldheaded; exactly the type that Erica liked. He wasn't as thick as she liked her men, but she knew he was the one for her.

Troy was probably just their homeboy, and he really wasn't much to look at. He had frizzy cornrows, buck teeth, and wore a wack ass Karl Kani outfit. He was sagging his pants way too hard, they were almost to his knees. He had a nice red complexion, but the acne on his face was a major turn off for CeCe. However, he was perfect for Destiny. Last, but definitely not least, was the white boy of the crew. He was the handsome football star, Kevin. Kevin had always been down with black people. His hair was cut into a flat top with two parts on the left side, and his baby blue eyes mesmerized CeCe. Erica didn't even give Kevin a second look, but he made CeCe's pussy throb.

"Yeah, ya'll gon' pay for ours too when we order yours?" CeCe answered zeroing in on Kevin. She was letting the other two clowns know she was checking for him.

"Of course," Kevin gave his signature smirk.

"You know who you look like?" CeCe asked, and then answered her own question. "Vanilla Ice," she giggled.

"Yeah a lot of people say that," he laughed while stepping up to pay for their items.

"Umm, he is a sexy ass white boy! I'm 'bout to get his number and get me some of that white cock," CeCe thought as she admired his 6'1" frame. *"I bet he got a big one, ummm mm"*

****

"What's good Bruh?" Tony asked stepping up to give Chuck some dap, "Sorry to see what happened to your mom."

"It's all good Blood," he answered giving him the signature Blood handshake. "I know ya'll came by to ask about Hakeem," he said before turning to give the secret handshake to Harold. "What's good Blood?" he said to Harold.

"Ain't shit, yeah you know we wanna know what happened to Keem. That was crazy," Harold paused, "Oh yeah, sorry about your moms."

"Ya'll come in," Chuck opened the screen door; "We can smoke and talk."

He watched the two as they walked in, studying their facial movements and hoped they didn't come with the same intentions that Hakeem had. He had already endured as much bullshit as he could stand. He watched them take a seat, and then he slid to his room to tuck his .40 cal in his waistband. He looked in the mirror to make sure it was covered, and then went out to have a conversation with Tony and Harold.

"Yeah man," Chuck started as he walked in the living room, "Hakeem came through tripping. I was in the room and he came in and tried to pull the strap on me."

"Word?" Tony asked. He wrinkled his forehead, sending freckles running around on his red complexion. "What the fuck was wrong with him?"

Chuck shrugged, "I guess 'cause the police came and picked me up yesterday to ask me some questions."

"Questions about what," Harold came from the sideline with worry evident in his voice.

"Not about the murder, they were trying to say I killed this other dude."

"Who?" Tony jumped back in.

"This dude named Brett, anyway that was some bullshit so they brought me back and Keem was outside. He came over, asked me about the police, and he tried to kill me. I guess he thought I was gon' snitch on him, but what would make him think that?"

"I don't know. This is the first I heard of this. You know how the projects talk; they said you killed Keem cause of some chick." Tony continued.

"Come on now, you know I ain't trippin on no bitch?"

"I don't know Blood; I'm just telling you what they told me."

"Word, well that's some bullshit. And now my mom is dead," Chuck put his head down trying to fight the tears.

"What you gon' do now?" Harold asked.

"I don't know, but I'm 'bout to get my shit and get the fuck up outta here. Ya'll gon' help me get my stuff together?"

"Yeah come on," they filed into Chuck's room to start packing.

****

"So what school do you go to?" Kevin asked looking into CeCe's pretty brown eyes.

"Carver, and you?"

"I go to North; I'm the quarterback of the football team. You play any sports?"

"Nah, I do like to practice with the cheerleaders sometimes; the coach is a friend of my dad's and I have a friend who cheers."

"Cool, so that means you can come to my game next Friday?"

"Maybe I can do that, I'd like to see you play. We gon' get up afterwards?" CeCe smirked as she sensually licked her full lips.

"Yeah, we gon' definitely get up," Kevin smiled, once again making her pussy moist.

While she was flirting and making googly eyes at Kevin, not one time did the name Chuck cross her mind. However, she was heavily on his. CeCe liked Chuck, but she loved sex. The more people she had sex with, the more she was addicted to having random sex. She was quickly developing a destructive habit, and never once thought that any of her actions could catch up to her. She was living her life for moments of pleasure.

Chapter 11

Chuck spent the next few days with his aunt while he looked for an affordable apartment. The stress of losing his mother was physically draining him, and the fact that the police said that they suspected foul play had his mind searching for suspects. After the autopsy was performed on his mother's body, her death was officially ruled a homicide.

Chuck was bothered most by the fact that he could have had a hand in his mother's murder. He was having irrational thoughts which made him grow distant. He started missing school on a regular basis. He couldn't really focus on classes anymore; he had to stand on his own and take care of himself. When he wasn't plotting his course of action, he was thinking about CeCe. He had only talked to her two times since his mother's death, but he was starting to seriously miss her. He did like the fact that she respected his wishes when he told her he didn't feel like talking much.

CeCe, of course, wasn't sitting around moping. She and Kevin had been having late night phone conversations, many of them involving phone sex. Kevin was a smooth talker, and his parents definitely raised him to respect women. CeCe was turned off by the fact that Chuck was slacking from school. She had plans of going off to college and pursuing her dream. Kevin was an academic and athletic All-American; he had a brighter future than Chuck, in CeCe's mind. Yet she still had a thing for Chuck, and had no plans to stop having sex with him. She also knew she was going to give Kevin some the first chance she got. She had pretty much forgotten all about Brett, but the police hadn't.

****

Police Station

"How close are we to finally putting the finishing touches on Brett's murder?" Detective Brown asked Martinez.

"The tire match should be here as soon as Friday. The gun came back stolen, but guess who left a print on the shell?"

"Let me guess, Chuck Jenkins?"

"Nope, you were way off with that one."

"The father?"

"Yes sir, and when the tires match the tire marks left at the scene we can go pick him up and charge him with murder."

"Not before I get a confession out of him," Detective Brown said firmly.

"Friday should be the day."

"What about Chuck's mother? Who killed her?"

"We're still investigating that murder, but there were finger prints lifted from the scene. There was semen found inside her too, so we should be able to find the perp," Martinez boasted letting his boss know that he was working hard.

"Any luck on those two gang bangers from Cali?" Brown added.

"No, no leads as of yet, but we're still working on it."

"So many bodies stacking up, you think we're losing control over the city?"

"I hope not, but we have to solve these murders and give these families peace of mind. It's our job."

****

"Hello?" CeCe answered the phone after the first ring.

"Hey Baby!" Chuck spoke into the receiver.

She rolled her eyes, but put on a fake smile, "Hey Chuck, what you been up to?"

"Ain't shit, just getting myself together. I just got an apartment, and I went to Rent a Center and got a bedroom suit, living room suit, and a big screen TV so we can watch movies when you come over."

"You got your own place now? Wow, that's good. When is your mom's funeral?"

"It's Friday, but it's not really a funeral-they gon' cremate her. I bought an urn to put her ashes in to keep forever."

"That's creepy, that's not gon' make you have nightmares?"

"Nah, it's cool to me. I'll have somebody to talk to when I don't have nobody to talk to."

CeCe looked at the phone and shook her head, "Oh, well that's cool. I guess maybe we can catch up this weekend."

"Yeah, why don't you come through Friday?"

"Friday I have to go to my friend's mom's banquet. I wish I could be there, but I have a prior engagement."

"It's all good."

"Well, I'm gon' call you back ok?"

"Aight."

CeCe hung up the phone and went to go talk to her father about her plans for the weekend.

"Daddy," she poked her head into his room.

"Yeah Pumpkin?"

"I wanna go spend the weekend with Erica and Destiny," she said giving him her most innocent look.

"Now didn't I tell you I don't like you hanging out with Destiny," he cut his eyes at his daughter while he watched TV.

"Daddy," she said in a sad pleading tone, "She's not a bad influence on me, I'm a good girl and I don't have friends that are bad."

"Yeah right. You were just pregnant, so you can kill the innocent act Missy."

"Daddy pleeeaaaasssseee," she begged.

"Have you already talked to her mom?"

"Yes, I would be going straight over there after school Friday."

Vernon sighed and gave in to her whining. "Ok fine, but I'm coming to get you early Sunday so we can go visit your mother's grave. Deal?"

"Deal!" she excitedly said, "You're the best dad in the whole wide world!"

****

While Chuck patiently waited for the movers to bring the furniture over, he posted up by his window and lit a blunt. He was still wrapping his mind around that $2,000 that he spent to get his own place. There were still some minor things that had to be done, like switching the lights and the water bills to his name. He could wait a few days on that though. His funds were starting to run low. Chuck wanted to give his mother a funeral with a nice casket and a church full of her friends to come to see her before she was buried. He then questioned if anyone would even care enough ,to show up.

His mom never dealt with her brothers and sisters, and Chuck didn't even remember them. He knew all of her so called boyfriends didn't care about either her or him. He put up with lots of shit from her abusive men, some used to beat him like a grown man. He suffered many nosebleeds and black eyes from some of them. His mother never stopped the vicious attacks, most of the time she was too strung out to care. The first time Chuck murdered someone was when he was ten years old. He recalled the incident in his mind as he watched the cars roll by.

FLASHBACK

"You stupid bitch! Where you been? Out with that damn Frank all night haven't you," Johnny, his mother's boyfriend spat. His hand mashed the side of her face and she fell to the kitchen table sending the salt and pepper shakers and hot sauce flying to the floor. He grabbed her by the back of her head, wrapping her hair in his left fist, and began pounding her with his right.

"Get off my mom!" Young Chuck ran from the living room in a feeble attempt to save his mother. He ran into a stiff right hand to his left eye that knocked him out cold. The next thing he remembered was the cold water splashed in his face. He woke thinking he was drowning.

As he came around, his sight started coming back. He saw his mom's hand tap his cheek and heard her voice, "Wake up baby."

"What happened to your face momma?" Young Chuck reached up and rubbed his hands across his mother's swollen and bruised face. She was black and blue and trickling red.

"Momma, you gon' call an ambulance?"

"Nah baby, momma ok," she spoke from the side of her mouth. She was barely able to part her lips; they were three sizes larger than normal due to the savage beating.

He helped his mother nurse her wounds while peeking out of the one good eye. Although his vision was damaged, it still hurt him to see his mother like that. She may not have been the best mother, but she was all he had. Later, when his mom went to sleep, he reached under the mattress and grabbed the fully loaded black .38 snub nose and stuffed it in the waistband of his jeans.

He had one good eye, but that was all he needed to walk through the projects and find that bastard Johnny Nicholson. Chuck would always see him going in and out of different women's houses, so he just had to walk around and find the right one. It didn't take too long, when he heard his voice escaping from the screen door of some lady's porch. He knew her by sight, but had never spoken to her.

He began his approach; his heart began speeding up and pounded in his chest like it was trying to escape.

Chuck kept moving. The closer and closer he got, the more his blood began to boil. He gritted his teeth while walking up the stairs to the project porch. There he was, with his back turned arguing at the almond brown woman. The butterflies felt like they were migrating south into the pit of his stomach, but his mind was made up. He was about to watch Johnny take his last breath for beating he and his mom.

Chuck snatched the screen door open, and made his way into the house. He startled Johnny and his female companion, who was looking thick and rather sexy. They turned and looked in his direction with puzzled looks. He shut the door, locked it, and turned back to look at the two from his one open eye.

"What the fuck you doing?" Johnny drunkenly belted.

"The same shit you do," Chuck answered. He released the pistol from his waistband, gripped the handle, and placed his finger on the trigger. He aimed at Johnny's head.

"What the fuck you gon' do with that? You bett…" were his last words as the .38 slug ripped through his forehead and blew his brains on the wall behind him. The lady got half a scream out before two slugs pounded her chest, and her lifeless body fell to the floor beside Johnny's.

"No good, cheating ass muthafucka," Chuck said as he stared at the bodies with no remorse. His first murder scene set the tone for the rest of his life.

"Young Blood," a deep gravelly voice startled him out of his trance.

"What's up?" He turned around and eyed the fairly short, dark brown, baldheaded figure walking up the stairs toward him. He realized the old head was the other occupant of the small building.

"I see you just moved in earlier," the man extended his hand. Chuck returned his and they shook.

"Yeah, I just moved in. What's up with this spot? I know we're close to the money, and shit be moving on this side of town." Chuck figured he would throw that shit out there to see what dude was all about.

"Damn, you move fast young brother. How you know I ain't police?"

"Cause you didn't look like a cop, and what's the odds of a cop living in some shit like this?"

"Shit like this? What's wrong with this place?" the man asked. He was obviously a little offended.

"I mean, the units aren't filled up and it's not like people lining up to wanna live here. This ain't no place for a cop. What's your name anyway mister?"

"Blaze, and yours?

"C-Roy," Chuck answered. He decided it was time to get a nick name; he was tired of his name and wanted a new start to go with the new him. His mom was dead now, and at eighteen he had to fend for himself. He had to become a man before he even fully understood what manhood was all about.

"Well C-Roy, I guess since the secret is out that I'm not a cop, you won't mind me doing this," Blaze reached into his front pocket and pulled out a Newport box and opened it. There were two cigarettes, a red lighter, and a stem. When he dumped the contents in his hand, the buttery brown piece of crack plopped in the center of his palm. Blaze had no shame; he placed the crack at the top of a glass pipe with a black smut tint. He leaned his head back, flicked the lighter causing flames to shoot high and put the stem to his lips. He let the flame sizzle the crack and took a deep breath. Blaze held the smoke in, shook his head like he was agreeing that the crack in the stem was the best thing since sliced bread.

Chuck shook his head and sat watching this dumb ass old coon get high in front of him. When the light colored smoke emerged from Blaze's lips, the smell made him cringe and cover his mouth. He said, "Damn that shit stank." Blaze didn't care what he was saying, he was in his zone and his eyes were set immediately on high beam. Chuck had never really seen anybody smoke crack, he just sold pieces to people and went on about his business.

Blaze's face looked beat down by crack, and he looked every bit of sixty years old with his salt and pepper Jherri curl and matching goatee. The craters in his face told tales of unkept skin. Chuck thought, "*There's no way I can smoke crack.*" But as long as people were buying, he was selling. Chuck only cared about money, and now CeCe.

****

CeCe was only thinking about Friday night with Kevin and his boys, and her girls. She had been talking and having phone sex with Kevin all week, while dodging Chuck's calls. She answered every now and then, but she wasn't really checking for him. She wanted something new; white dick was on her mind.

CeCe had been hooked on sex from an early age. The first dick penetrated her cervix at thirteen.

One day she was walking down her street past Mr. G's house. Mr. G was an older man who lived in the neighborhood and preyed on the young girls. On this summer day, CeCe was looking good and she knew it. Mr. G called to her as she walked past on the way to the store in her little booty shorts. She went over to see what he wanted. One thing led to another, and he wound up digging in her virgin guts. He pounded her like a grown woman. CeCe was in the bed screaming and bleeding all over his sheets, but he didn't care. He loved young, tight pussy.

He ravaged her, and humped her senseless. He ripped her innocence from her and introduced her body to orgasms before it's time. She took the dick as best she could, but almost lost her mind when she came. In retrospect, Mr. G really wasn't that big to her now compared to other dicks that she had ridden. CeCe surmised that he preyed on young girls because his dick wasn't equipped for a grown woman. She quickly outgrew his small penis and started having sex whenever she could.

CeCe became a sex addict on that day, and she started fucking this dude and that dude, and that other dude too. Lately she had been looking at her friends differently, and she was longing to have sex with a female. She felt she couldn't let that secret out because she didn't want to alienate her girls.

Dudes and chicks were coming up during these times. It was the middle of the crack era, and big money and big jewelry were sure signs of a baller. She loved all the tricked out cars that the local dope boys were pushing. Especially the Toyotas and Hondas hooked up with the deep dish hammers, and the all of the BMW's. They looked like rappers walking around the city, and she always wanted one of those dudes. Mr. G had her creeped out on older men, so she mostly stuck with the boys her age. She was determined to find a baller though and put that pussy on him. Until then, she was gon' practice until her skills were perfect.

Chuck, on the other hand, was not really on her radar. He and CeCe were cut from similar cloths, they both had checkered pasts. As the old saying goes, "You never know who you meet until you meet them." Chuck was sold on CeCe from the moment she said spoke to him. Unfortunately, she didn't immediately feel the same way. She wouldn't have given him any conversation if he didn't flash the cash. Chuck couldn't see that, her smile was warm and her ass was captivating.

Yeah, the two of them had sex, but so what. CeCe had been given plenty of pipe before he laid his. Chuck had a good sex game, but so did many other dudes. She wasn't ready to be exclusive. Chuck really wasn't either, but he did consider CeCe as his main girl. He was including her in his future plans. Friday, November 10, 1992 was going to mark the beginning of their future.

Chapter 12

Friday morning began like any other day when the moon took a break. The glowing orange and red sphere illuminated the sky as the sun climbed the horizon from the east. The rays danced around CeCe's room, forcing her to crack her eyelids slowly while the alarm clock tapped on her eardrums. She grudgingly arose from the bed and stretched her sleeping muscles while sitting on the edge. She planted her feet on the ground and dragged herself over to the clock to hit the snooze button. Seeing her image in the mirror made her smile to herself; she knew tonight her and the girls were getting up with Kevin and his boys. Her clit rang in between her legs like a dinner bell, and tonight she was serving up that ass to Kevin.

"I'm gon' put that thang on that white boy. I bet he got a big pink cock," CeCe said softly to the mirror and started chuckling at herself. She made her way to the bathroom to shed the sleep from her skin with a fresh bar of soap. She grabbed a face cloth, body cloth, and a towel so she could get started on her daily bathing ritual. CeCe always made sure she kept that punanee clean and shaven. She couldn't have the boys munching on frizzy, smelly carpet. She heard white boys eat the best pussy in the world, and she wanted to make sure her's was fresh enough to ride Kevin's face tonight.

She peeled back the shower curtains and turned the water to hot. She shed her clothes on the floor and draped the towel over the toilet before getting in. The water doused her body as the steam rose from the shower. While she had her foot up on the edge of the tub washing her goodies, her other washcloth fell in the basin. She didn't know it until she dropped the one she was using beside it and couldn't tell which was which, since they were both red.

"Shit!" She looked down cursing herself. She had no idea which one to use. "Oh well," she shrugged. Of course she ended up washing her body with the face cloth and her face with the ass cloth. Either way, she still came out so fresh and so clean. This was actually the first sign that she was going to have a bad day, but she didn't know it yet.

****

The sun couldn't make its' way through the thick black sheets draped over the window in Chuck's room. His room didn't have the same life flowing through the walls as CeCe's. He was in a deep sleep when the alarm clock went off. Chuck hadn't been to school all week due to his situation, and really didn't want to go back and play catch up.

He was a man now; sleeping under his own roof, and lounging on furniture he had paid for. His money was getting low, but he had just enough to cop three ounces of raw, pay to get the house phone on, and still have money to buy groceries with pots and pans to go with them. The only remnants of his mother would be her ashes. He needed be at the funeral home at 7:00 PM tonight to retrieve them. The clock read 9:30 AM and Chuck knew the money didn't sleep. He let Blaze get a free twenty piece last night, and he hadn't been to sleep. His fist pounding the wooden door startled Chuck, and he jumped up to see who was there.

"Who is it?" Chuck called out in a sleepy angry voice.

"It's me Young Blood, Blaze, from downstairs. I need to holla at ya!!!" Blaze sang from the other side of the door. He was happy that he didn't have to drive across town to get some good crack.

Chuck opened the door still in his boxers and asked, "So what you need?"

"I got me a few friends over ya dig, and the white girl I got down there spends heavy. I'm starting off with a hundred, and she got plenty more to go. Make sure you put me in there now, 'cause I'm gon' spend my money wit ya."

"Aight Bruh, hold up," Chuck shut the door, and went to the room the retrieve the last seven grams of buttery brown pieces of crack chopped up in twenties. He also had some five and ten dollar rocks and a little shake at the bottom of the bag. He would take change when the heads come through after they had spent all their money. Chuck wasn't turning down a dollar, and he knew what fifty cent meant. Two fifties made a dollar, and he didn't discriminate on the pennies either; they made dollars too. Money was the motive, and Chuck was all about his paper.

He grabbed six twenty dollar rocks and took them back to Blaze, who was all fidgety and jittery-a true sign of a crack head. The monkey was on his back hard, and the shit Chuck had was that straight drop-the purest form of crack in the streets at the time. Timing was everything when you were taking over, or building up a block. The product surrounding this little unit was nothing like what Chuck was whipping up, and his connect in the Circle Projects kept the best shit in town. Not a lot of dealers could deal straight with a connect, but Chuck wasn't your average hustler. He had been a G since the age of eight, and his street rep was steadily building. From the murder he committed at ten years old, to those two bloods he burnt up in that house, the streets were talking. Chuck's name was ringing bells, and people knew that he was not the one to test. No one would snitch on him because he was guaranteed to make bond and come handle his business.

The 90's were booming and the crack game was major. Cocaine was the most popular drug in Winston-Salem, and crack moved faster than running water. It didn't take long for Chuck to start making some real money; he was well on his way.

Chuck hopped in the shower, and started to get ready for his day. First, he had to go get his phone turned on. Then, he was headed to Page 2000 to scoop up a new pager. He wanted to get a new cell phone too, but decided he could wait on that one. Finally, he wanted to hit the grocery store to buy food and some cooking supplies.

****

"Daddy, you gon' take me to school?" I don't feel like riding the bus," CeCe asked Vernon as he walked into the house.

"Yeah, I can drop you off at school. What's the overnight bag for?" Vernon asked, obviously concerned about the Adidas bag hanging from her left shoulder.

"You don't remember Daddy? I'm going to spend the night with Erica tonight. She's coming to pick me up after school, and I'll be home on Sunday," CeCe smiled.

"Oh no young lady, I'll be over there to pick you up Saturday morning. I changed my mind; you're not staying away all weekend, no way."

"Fine Daddy," CeCe gave in to defeat, she was just happy for the night out. "Let's go, I'm ready."

Without missing a beat, Vernon turned around to drop her off at school. He didn't have to warm up the car since he had just shut the engine off. They both hopped in and headed off to school; neither of them noticed the dark blue Ford Taurus trailing behind. Vernon and CeCe made small talk and joked with each other on the way.

Detective Brown and Martinez had been following Vernon since he got off work that morning. They were waiting for the judge to wake up and sign the search warrant so they could arrest him on a murder charge. Brown hated the fact that the evidence didn't point to Chuck. But due to the unexpected turn of events, he was still able to nail Chuck on the manslaughter charge.

The officers patiently watched as he pulled into the parking lot and dropped his daughter off. CeCe was so happy that she was going out tonight that she didn't recognize the detectives, who were two cars down from theirs. Vernon pulled off and headed back to the house. The confirmation of the warrant came minutes later, and the Taurus sped around the two cars separating them and hopped in behind Vernon. They hit the lights and sirens and were happy to finally be able to take Vernon into custody. He looked in the rearview mirror and hissed, "Shit." He veered off to the side of the road and put the car in park. His mind was racing as he waited for the officers to approach. The two detectives walked up to both sides of the car with their hands on their holstered weapons.

"Officers, can I help you?" Vernon rolled down the window and looked over his shoulder. He recognized the same cop who came to pick up his daughter for questioning.

"Sir, I'm going to need you to turn your car off with your right hand and put your left hand out the window. Slowly take the keys from the ignition and drop them on the ground.

"What?"

"Just do it, sir! I'll explain soon enough," Brown instructed, pulling his firearm from the holster and holding it at his side.

Vernon followed the instructions, and dropped the keys. Brown placed the 9mm in his holster, grabbed his handcuffs, and cuffed Vernon's left hand. He then opened the door and got him out of the car, and placed his arms behind his back and cuffed his wrists.

"You are under arrest for the murder of Brett Wallace. You have the right to remain silent. Anything said can and will be used against you in a court of law. You have the right to an attorney, if you can't afford one, one will be appointed to you. Do you understand your rights?" Brown asked him. Vernon shook his head yes in response. Martinez called for a tow truck to come and impound the car for evidence. They put Vernon in the back of the squad car and they headed to the station.

****

Chuck paid for his phone service to be activated, and had already picked up his new pager before he stopped at the pay phone to call his connect Will-G. He and Will had met through a mutual acquaintance, and shit had been on ever since. He decided to stop and get a blunt since Will told him the shipment hadn't quite made it yet, but it was on the way.

Usually he would wait until his connect was straight, but today he had time to chill and wait. This was a definite sign to him that he was coming up. He finally had a chance to deal with a real G who was making the type of money that he wanted to see.

He pulled into the housing project and in front of the spot where Will told him to meet him. Will was never in one exclusive apartment, he had spots all over the hood. He was like the king snake, everybody looked out for him. The police were never going to get a lead on Will, he never sat still.

"What up Bruh!" Will said. He smiled and flashed a mouth full of gold teeth. His dark brown, almost black, complexion reminded Chuck of Wesley Snipes. His nose was just as full as his lips, and he wore his hair in cornrows. He always had on tank tops as if he just finished working out. He loved to flex his muscles and let dudes know that trying him wouldn't be easy.

"What's good Blood," Chuck dapped him up while walking into the house. The heat in the projects was on 1000, and Chuck had to remove the Triple Fat Goose he sported.

"You grab them cigars?"

"Yeah, I got em," Chuck reached into his coat pocket to produce the two White Owl blunts.

Will threw him a bag of some kind of weed; he sat down and split the blunt and dumped the cigar guts inside the trash. He began to lick the blunt so he could fill it, twist it, and fire it up. Chuck looked around the apartment; he saw pictures of some chocolate honey and her kids. He assumed that this was her house, but he really didn't care. The two sat and conversed about up and coming moves they were about to make. Will was about to front him three ounces since he was buying three, but also because Chuck had come up. He had been buying steady for some time now, and his money never came up short. Also, he never bought less than what he bought on his previous visit. He proved that he was ready to step his game up. Chuck's life was about to start moving really fast. He was only focused on stacking paper; he couldn't see that his world was about to close in on him. Life as he knew it was changing, and his heart was lost in the wrong forest of love.

****

CeCe's eyes lit up as Erica pulled up in her 1992 shiny black Honda Accord, with 18" rims. She grabbed her bag and threw it in the backseat and hopped in the front.

"Hey girl! Your car is looking good!"

"Thanks, I just got it washed yesterday. And I got two tens and an amp in the trunk. Listen while I pump this new Snoop," Erica told her friend and turned up the Alpine. *"You're back now at the Jack off hour, this is DJ Eazy Dick..."* started through the speakers as the beat dropped for "Aint No Fun if the Homies Can't Have None." The two rode together jamming to the music.

"So you talked to Kevin?" Erica asked turning the music down a little.

"Yeah, I've been talking to him all week girl," CeCe exclaimed, "I can't wait 'til tonight. I'm gone put that thang on his ass. What about you? You talked to Mr. Tall, Dark and Handsome?"

"Hell yeah! While you bullshitting, we gon' all be fucking tonight. I can't wait to see what he working with. I need some good dick in my life."

"Girl, I had some good dick lately that I know would be the bomb if we had time to ourselves."

"What haven't you told me?" Erica looked over at her friend who was glowing.

"Well, this dude Chuck I met, he has some good dick. He's a good dude too because I had to go to the hospital when Brett beat me up, and he stayed with me. I never really had a dude care about me like that," CeCe got lost in her thoughts.

"Brett jumped on you? You know he dead right?"

"Yeah, I know. He died the same night that happened to me."

"What!" Erica gave her friend a surprised look.

"Yep, they still don't know who did it."

****

Detectives Brown and Simpson entered the interrogation room and took a seat. "So, I'm sure you know why you're here. What's your side of the story?"

"The side of what story?" Vernon asked calmly. He was trying to hide the fact that his heart was rapidly beating and he could feel his blood pressure rising.

"Now we're going to play dumb?" Brown said, but he was cut off by Simpson. "I'm not about to play this cat and mouse game. We have a dead kid," she pulled a photo of Brett out of her folder and laid it in front of him.

Vernon looked at the picture and sighed, "He hurt my daughter," he began as tears started to flow from his eyes. "I overreacted. When I saw my child lying in that hospital bed and the doctor told me she lost a baby-my grandchild, it did something to me. No, I didn't want to be a grandfather just yet, but I accept all new life."

Vernon gave a slight pause to gather his emotions. Brown decided to keep digging, "So the fact that he killed your grandchild and hurt your daughter made you do what?"

"I killed him," Vernon placed his face in his hands, "I shot him."

Detective Simpson and Brown got what they were looking for and it was much easier than they thought it would be. They decided to let him sit and think about what he had done before they processed him.

****

Chuck went back to his crib and stashed five ounces; he decided to cook one up. He knew how to stretch the coke to bring back more crack than usual. He was getting ounces for the low, so he cooked up twenty-eight grams back to twenty-five grams. He lost three grams in the cooking process, but it didn't matter. His product was better, and that allowed him to sell smaller pieces. Chuck believed in quality over quantity.

The word was quickly getting around about his product. The knocks on his door started coming more frequently. Chuck's money was quickly stacking. He hustled past the time he allotted to go grocery shopping, and the time crept up on him before he knew it. It was now time to go pay his final respects to his mother. He still hadn't gotten over the fact that she was gone, but he couldn't do anything about it.

He threw on a white button down shirt, a pair of black slacks, his Stacy Adams wingtips, and a black tie to accent the look. He threw on his Polo frames, although the sun was laying itself to rest in the west. Chuck was ready to put his mother's death behind him as he hopped in the car and headed out. When he arrived at the funeral home, he noticed Detective Martinez standing outside. He wanted to flee, but he had no reason to do so. He hadn't done anything, well not that the police were aware of.

"What you doing here?" Chuck asked, while walking towards Martinez.

"I came to ask you a few questions."

"About what? And why you come when I'm trying to bury my mother?"

"That's the thing, it's about your mom. We have been looking for you, and you were nowhere to be found. Now, about your mother…"

"What about her?" Chuck cut him off.

"Her death was officially ruled a homicide."

"What?" Chuck's nose flared and his forehead wrinkled up.

"Yes your mother was murdered. We were wondering if you know anything about it."

"Muthafucka what you asking? Did I kill my mom?"

"No, but we wanna know who was out to hurt her."

Chuck's eyes were looking through the detective when he said, "You better find out before I do, or you gon' be toe tagging that bitch," and stormed off.

Chapter 13

The lights illuminated the football field and the raucous crowd was deafening. Students, alumni, and community members were all in the stands and scattered about the stadium. Parkland High School was playing North Forsyth; this was the annual city rivalry game. Troy and Jay met CeCe, Erica, and Destiny in the parking lot. The girls were certainly looking good in their tight jeans with thermals underneath, puffy coats, sweaters, and scarves draped around their necks. They all also sported toboggans and snow boots. It was abnormally cold, and they were dressed for the weather.

The wind was slicing through most of the crowd, but these three ladies and two fellas had it together. The only member missing was Kevin, and he was out on the field. The group made a pit stop at the concession stand. They ordered hot chocolate, nachos, and candy; they were ready to sit down and watch Kevin do his thing. CeCe was overly excited to see Kevin on the field. He was bragging to her about his skills on the field, so she wanted to see them in person. He was headed to college on a full football scholarship, which had already been awarded- unbeknownst to CeCe. The only thing she wanted was to get him alone tonight.

She was totally enthralled in her own thoughts when she walked by Chuck and didn't even notice him. He was in the parking lot serving some of his clients from North Forsyth. Since he had the best shit floating, Chuck was all over town. Initially he was there to handle business, but seeing CeCe smiling with these two dudes made him jealous. He figured he would make his presence known to see how she would act in front of her friends. He paid for his ticket at the front gate and ventured inside.

Finally, he came across CeCe's smile. Her face was intensely focused on the game. She wasn't booed up with either of the two guys, Chuck was a little puzzled. He figured she was just a football fan, so he began his climb up the bleachers to make his presence known.

"What's up CeCe?" Chuck's voice and smiling face threw her equilibrium off and she had to think about what was happening.

"Hey Chuck, what you doing here?" CeCe dryly replied. She sounded extremely nervous. Chuck picked up on her uncomfortable response and the shiftiness of her body.

"I had to come holla at my peoples. What's good Jay?" he turned to dap Jay. "What's up Tony?" then turned and dapped Tony up.

"Cool, what's up" CeCe said.

"Nothing, I came to give you my new pager number," he pulled out a piece of paper that already contained his number and handed it to her.

"Oh okay, thanks," she gave a fake smile, then jumped up when Kevin threw a 60 yard touchdown pass.

Chuck didn't like being ignored, so turned around to leave before he lost control of his hand and it tasted her left cheek. After all that time sitting with her at the hospital, she was gon' play him like this. He felt he should've treated her like the bitch she acted like. The farther he walked, the madder he got-that is until she stopped him in the parking lot...

"Chuck, wait!" A sexy southern belle called out as he was making his way to the car.

"Who dat?" Chuck asked. He couldn't make out the voice and his vision was obstructed by several people in front of him.

"Oh, you don't remember me now?" The pretty, milk chocolate skinned female finally came into his eyesight. It was Precious' sexy ass.

The two met some time ago, back around the time he and Hakeem had first met. She was just as sexy now as she was on the first night they met. Precious was like a bag of M&M's; she melted in his mouth. He loved to dive in between her legs face first and gobble her clit. She was from Atlanta and had a slick B-Girl swag. All of her brothers were drug dealers and murderers, so she was deep in the game herself.

She migrated to Winston-Salem about four years ago, and the first person she met was Chuck. The two of them were never exclusive, but one day Chuck got in his feelings and decided he was going to beat her ass. Unfortunately for him, it didn't turn out the way he expected. It was two years ago when they fell out. He was only sixteen and she was twenty-five. Precious was what many people today call a cougar.

Her curves were dangerous on that 5'7" frame. She had an ass that you could sit a drink on and thighs that would make KFC jealous. To top it all off, she was bowlegged and pigeon-toed. Two years later, she looked better than Chuck remembered.

"What's been up wit' you?" she asked.

"Nothing, my mom just died and was cremated today. What you doing back in these parts?"

"Wow, sorry to hear that. I've been back for about a week now. You know my lil brother play for Parkland. I figured I would come with my mom and check him out. I'm really not feeling this though, and I'm cold. Where are you headed?"

"Come on, get in the car and warm up," Chuck opened the door for her. While he was on the way to the other side of the car, she unlocked the door for him. Precious had deep feelings for Chuck, but he was too young for her to take seriously in those days. He started the car and turned the heat on low until it warmed up.

"So, what you been up to?" she asked. "You still trying to put your hands on women?"

"Nah, I aint about all that. I'm sorry that happened between us, I don't know what got into me."

"Oh you know it's cool, I had to beat yo ass though. You can't be trying to put your hands on females. That's why I had to cut you off. You grown now and you done got a little bigger. Is that pipe even longer now that you legal?" she flirted.

"Why don't you come to my crib and find out," Chuck quickly came back.

"Oh you got your own crib now?" Precious shockingly asked. "When did you get that?"

"Right after my mom passed. I had to get my own shit. I couldn't sleep in that house anymore."

"Why not?" Precious inquired.

Chuck didn't know how to tell her that he murdered Hakeem, but he never lied to her. He figured he would tell her what happened. "Man, Hakeem," he looked down. Precious sensed something was wrong. She lifted his chin so she could look into his eyes and said, "What happened to Hakeem baby?"

"He's dead."

"What?" she seemed genuinely stunned at the news, "What happened?"

"He tried to kill me, and we struggled over the gun. I finally got control of it and had to shoot him. I keep having nightmares about it," Chuck lied. He hadn't missed a wink of sleep, except to make money.

"Wow, that's crazy. You two were so close. I wonder what could make him wanna do something like that?"

"Who knows," Chuck shrugged. His pager went off and the code 808 let him know that Blaze was out of what he left for him to sell. He needed to get back to the crib to provide more supply for the heavy demand. "You with me?"

"Of course, I need some good dick," Precious flashed her pearly whites which seemed to glow in the dark.

****

Destiny, CeCe, Erica, Jay, and Troy all sat waiting for Kevin to come out of the locker room at North Forsyth in two different cars. Erica, CeCe, and Jay were all in Erica's car and Troy and Destiny were in his souped up RX-7 with a kit, spoiler, and chrome deep dish hammers. The car wore a flip flop paint job that changed colors while you looked at it. CeCe didn't know what Troy was into, but she was happy for her girl Destiny. She loved money just as much as CeCe did.

CeCe sat in the back leaning on the window. She was excited that she was finally about to spend some time with the Great White Hype. She thought about Chuck for a minute, but dismissed him from her mind quickly when Kevin strolled around the corner. He had a swagger that said "I know I'm the man." He played a phenomenal game. He threw six touchdown passes and rushed for two more.

"Hey you!" Kevin said as he opened the back door of Erica's ride.

She slid over quickly, cheesing from ear to ear and spoke, "Hey baby! Great game tonight," she sniffed him. She was thinking he was going to be funky, but he smelled shower clean. *"No wonder he took so long,"* she thought.

"Thanks baby," he said as he gave her a quick kiss.

"So what's up ya'll? Ya'll hungry? We can hit up Pizza Hut."

"Hell yeah my dude, Pizza Hut on a Friday night. Let's go!" Jay responded from the front seat.

"Yeah, I'm wit' it. What about you CeCe?" Erica turned to ask her friend.

"I wanna do whatever Kevin wants to do," she replied.

Kevin rolled down his window and called out to Troy, "Yo we goin' to Pizza Hut on University, across from the coliseum."

The cars rolled out and small talk went on in both vehicles as they headed to the spot. Everybody wore smiles and CeCe was ecstatic about chilling with Kevin. She was oblivious to the fact that her father was arrested earlier for murdering Brett. Her personal life was put on blast, and the entire Triad area: Winston-Salem, Greensboro, and High Point knew the details of the situation. Everybody except the people who were out at the football games saw the story, including Chuck and his old flame. They were at his crib sitting in the front of the TV screen watching the story run.

****

"Police have made an arrest in the case of Brett Wallace-the student from Carver High who was brutally murdered as he was walking home from the Carl Russell Recreation Center. Before Wallace played his last game of basketball, he allegedly physically attacked the daughter of Vernon White. In turn, he lost his life. Wallace was college bound, but his life was tragically cut short," the anchor woman on the news reported. Chuck watched in awe as the developing story aired. They even interviewed Brett's family and made the ordeal bigger than it was, in Chuck's eyes. He was going to put him under the dirt himself. He felt he would have gotten away with it if he did it.

There was a knock at the door as the two of them sat and watched. Chuck decided that he would give Blaze a pack so he could make some money and smoke good while he handled Precious. He didn't really care about CeCe's dad going to jail, but he cared about the brown bombshell waiting for him to come and set it off.

When he got back upstairs, Precious was already in his bed down to her panties and bra. The lamp in the corner provided a red light and the room was dim. A shimmering glow of chocolate sparkled and her 36C's sat perfectly in the black lace. Her camel toe was poking from the front of the black lace panties as she lay on the bed with one leg up.

Chuck turned on the Sony boom box and let the quiet storm shower the room with smooth grooves. He peeled his shirt off and tossed it to the floor. He then unbuttoned his pants and slid them off. He exposed his meat which pointed east; it was happy to see what was in his bed. He began his approach on top of her and crawled every inch of her body until they were face to face. Their lips locked in a passionate kiss.

Precious was older and more experienced; she taught Chuck how to please a grown woman. She moaned as he began to pop her bra loose, letting her full breasts break free from bondage. He began to suck her long dark nipples. He flicked his tongue and sucked them one by one as he gripped them both closely together. She felt that missile on her leg and couldn't wait to get it inside of her, but she didn't want to rush things.

Chuck felt her body trembling under his as he starting kissing softly down her belly. He tapped her abdomen with his lips until he reached the top of her panties. Taking them in between his teeth, he bit them and started pulling them down her thighs. The speaker sung, "*Slooooowww dannncee, ooooo, hey Mr. DJ, why don't you slow this party down*," and Chuck began to climb her thighs with the same kisses that got him from her breasts to her panties.

Precious was in total ecstasy right now. R. Kelly was singing in her ear while Chuck took her clit between his lips and began to suck on it, exactly the way she had taught him. He was doing such a great job down there that she grabbed his head with both hands and gyrated her hips as he sucked, licked, and played in her kitty kat. He began sliding two fingers around inside her rubbing her spot. He was driving her crazy! She was losing control of herself as she yelled out, "Oh my God!" Her eyes rolled in the back of her head and her body went into convulsions. He didn't let up, he kept on munching away.

****

The same song was playing across town as CeCe and Kevin were engaged in the same sexual acts. He was munching on her box like it was a box of Crunch and Munch. His face was glazed like a donut. His tongue was putting something on her lil ass. She was in total bliss. She grabbed his fine strands of hair and buried his face deeper into her kitty.

Kevin was so caught up in the moment that a rubber never crossed his mind. When he knew he had made her climax, he positioned himself on top of her and sunk his meat inside her dripping wet insides. He felt a sensation he had never felt before. Even though he hung with Jay and Troy, he had never been with a black girl before. Her hole was an out of this world experience for him.

CeCe wasn't as impressed with his package; he wasn't as big as Chuck. Once Kevin started tagging that ass, she was having second thoughts. He started to seriously pound on her walls. She was into it and gripping onto him for dear life. Kevin jumped up and down inside of her like he was auditioning for Michael Jackson's "Beat It" video. The music no longer mattered; they fucked like NWA was blasting through the speakers. Kevin represented in the pussy like he was *Straight outta Compton.*

The sounds of ooos and ahhhhs filled all the bedrooms of his parent's beautiful home. Destiny, CeCe, and Erica were having their vaginas stuffed with good penis. Everyone in the house was having multiple orgasms, but CeCe and Kevin were the only ones who didn't use a condom. Kevin even dropped his loads inside of CeCe three times before it was all said and done.

****

Chuck was digging Precious out, but he still worked to the soulful sounds that came from the speakers. He knew exactly how she liked it; she hated being fucked like a rabbit, fast and out of control. She loved the tortoise method, slow and deep strokes drove Precious to ecstasy. Chuck was delivering orgasm after orgasm as frequently as UPS packages. She stayed soaking wet and made a huge wet mark under her plump juicy ass as her feet touched his ears.

Chuck was soft on the inside, and the love making going on in his new apartment brought back feelings from way back when. At one point she had him turned out, but now that he was older, he was tearing her insides out the frame. He flipped her over flat on her stomach and placed her legs together. He sunk deep inside of her from the back. The love making session was over at this point. He deep stroked her on her belly and switched to seek and destroy mode.

Precious was gripping the bed sheets as he went in and out, tapping places inside her that he had never touched. "Fuck me baby! Fuck meeeeee!" She screamed in excitement as Chuck tore that ass up. He pulled her hair and nibbled on her neck; he remembered she liked it a little rough. He represented in the pussy.

Just when he thought he was done, he caught a second wind and stood up at the edge of the bed to begin to put the finishing touches on her. He started drilling her with that long, thick, chocolate dick and slapped her on her ass and pulled her hair until they both collapsed. They were sweaty, tired, and all fucked out. They both laid there huffing and puffing. Precious's legs were shaking; her insides were full of the load that Chuck dropped off.

As he listened to the music, he thought about CeCe and wondered how she took the news about her father. He still had a soft spot for her in his heart and he wanted to console her even though he was with Precious. He was so overwhelmed with good sex that he didn't even get up. He fell asleep with dried up cum and Precious' juices on his dick. After a while,

Precious got up and washed herself off. She came back and wiped him off while he slept. Then she began rocking the mic while he was sleep. Round two was underway.

****

"So where do you see yourself in five years?" Kevin asked as CeCe lay in his arms.

"I want to go to college and graduate within five years. Hopefully, I'll have a banging job like my father. He's spoiled me and my mother to death and I want to do the same for my child one day."

As CeCe said that, it dawned on Kevin that he skeeted all up in her and he was hoping that didn't come back to bite him in the ass. It never crossed his mind that he wasn't the first person to run up in CeCe raw, and that he was just one of two-or three if you counted Brett-who recently dropped semen off in her. Of course CeCe wasn't going to tell him, she had no reason to do so.

He got his, she got hers, and everything was good. She had no idea that her father was settled in at the Forsyth County Jail, or that her life would forever be affected by this single night of passion.

The fact that they were only teenagers was no excuse for them being so irresponsible, but it felt really good. Little did either of them know at the time, but one of them had just infected the other with the HIV virus.

****

Forsyth County Jail

The jail was dirty and crowded. It was an overall shit hole. The city had plans on building a new jail because of the violence and overcrowded small cells. The iron bars were obsolete and looked like something seen in the 1950's. The newer jails out of town were far more advanced and did away with the bars.

Vernon lay with his hands behind his head staring off into space. He couldn't believe that he was the one lying here, since he wasn't the one that fired that fatal shot. Yeah he was responsible for the death, but he didn't pull the trigger. He gave up the gun and his car, but he wasn't the one who carried out the hit.

He was having a moral dilemma. He admitted to the police that he murdered Brett for what he did to CeCe. He was covering up the fact that Caesar, Jesus' son, was the actual culprit. Even if he had told the truth, he would still be in jail. So would Caesar, and snitching on a Mexican drug lord's son-especially the leader of the Dragon Cartel, probably wasn't the smartest thing in the world to do. Trusting Caesar to dispose of the gun for him got him put between a rock and a hard place. He knew it wouldn't be long before he was visited by Jackie Jones, a high powered attorney from Atlanta who had been handling their cases for years. The last time he had to fight a case for Vernon was when CeCe was in diapers.

Not knowing what he was going to do, he simply replayed old memories in his mind to take the pain away. He always promised his daughter that he was going to be there to protect her. He kept replaying her smile and thinking about how he was supposed to pick her up in the morning…. That would never happen.

Chapter 14

CeCe awoke and looked at the time and started flipping out. "Oh Shit!" she jumped up suddenly.

"What's wrong?" Kevin unenthusiastically looked up. He was not happy about being disturbed so early.

"My dad is going to be coming to get me from Erica's house. He gon' bug out when he find out I'm not there," CeCe spoke fast while she was dressing herself.

Kevin watched her ass and titties bounce around while she was trying to hurry up and get dressed. He knew he didn't have to take her home, so he never got out of bed. He drifted back off to sleep.

"Erica, get up!!!" CeCe was knocking on the bedroom door that held Erica and Jay Jay.

"Whaaattttt?" Erica called out from the other side of the door.

"Come on girl, I got to get up out of here. My dad's coming to get me. Please!"

"Ok, I'm coming," Erica said. She slowly made her way out the bed.

CeCe repeated the same steps with Destiny, and everybody finally got up and got themselves together. The girls were dragging ass because the Absolut from last night was still creeping through their veins. Their brains were running in slow motion. Teenage girls, alcohol, and boys were any parent's nightmare. Kevin's parents would fall out and die if they knew their son took the whole black thing to this level and had sex with CeCe.

She definitely wouldn't be their type of girl. The photos on the wall screamed KKK and featured a photo of Kevin's uncle who was a skinhead. All CeCe cared about was getting some dick and getting her pussy licked. She never once looked at the pictures on the wall. She never even asked if he had a STD before she had unprotected sex with him. It probably wouldn't have mattered if she did ask, Kevin had no idea he was HIV positive. He had contracted the disease from his ex-girlfriend Karen. Karen and Kevin were together for about one year. They grew apart when Kevin started hanging out with Jay Jay and Troy. Karen was a suburban white girl who had no interest in black culture. She could not understand Kevin's fascination with it and decided to break up with him after asking him several times to stop hanging out with "the niggers."

What would Vernon think about his baby girl now? Especially after everything he had given up for her. He was sitting in a jail cell and she had just contracted HIV from a white boy.

****

The loud knock at the door awakened Chuck and Precious from their deep slumber, the kind that comes with the hot and steamy sex sessions they had throughout the night.

"Who is that baby?" Precious asked.

"Your guess is as good as mine. I'm 'bout to go see," Chuck said standing up and stretching.

"Well I hope you not going to the door swinging," she reached out and grabbed his dick.

"Nah," he laughed, "Imma slide somethin' on," he assured her and threw on some jogging pants. He grabbed his .45 as a precautionary measure; you could never be too careful in his line of work. He walked to the door and yelled, "Who is it?"

"Damn Blood, we had to hear about your new crib and shit?" Tony said from on the other side of the door.

Chuck made a 'come on son' face, he was pissed about being dragged out of bed because Tony was at the door. He knew he didn't tell anybody where he lived. *So how did he know where to find me,* Chuck thought to himself. He looked through the peephole, tucked the gun under his pillow on the couch, and opened the door. He needed answers.

****

"I wonder where my daddy is," CeCe turned and looked away from the 50" big screen TV. She was lounging on the sectional sofa and waiting for the news to come on. Erica was drinking coffee, still trying to shake the effects of last night. CeCe made sure they arrived back at her house before Vernon got off work and showed up to get her. Erica had to leave her new chocolate fling, but that's what friends were for; she made a sacrifice. "Never sell your girls out for no dick," was a motto their friendship was based on.

"He's coming, you already know that. Your daddy keep a close leash on you, and you be running around doing the most shit. I bet he don't even know you fucking," Erica spat. She unknowingly opened a can of worms.

"Yes he do, I was just pregnant, duhhh!" CeCe tried to stuff the words back inside her mouth, but it was too late.

"Pregnant?" Erica inquired, "You don't use condoms?"

"Yeah I use condoms girl, shitttttttt," she lied. "Ain't no way I'm gon' be fucking with no condom. The condom popped that night."

"So who were you pregnant by?" Erica curiously asked.

"The dude I told you about earlier, Brett. The one that beat me up and put me in the hospital, he kicked me in the stomach and I lost the baby. It wasn't a big deal."

Erica interrupted her.

"Wasn't a big deal!!!" Erica's words reeked of disgust. "CeCe you were pregnant," the girls were interrupted by the picture that flashed on the TV screen. It was Brett.

"Yesterday the killer of eighteen year old Brett Wallace was apprehended just a mile from the actual crime scene. Thirty-four year old Vernon White has been arrested and charged with First Degree Murder, but will also face charges in Miami, FL for a murder that occurred seven months back. The murder weapon, which was recovered, was linked to the murder of twenty-two year old Jose Gonzalez. White is being held in Forsyth County Detention Center without bond."

****

Tony slammed the .357 magnum to the side of Chuck's face sending him flying backwards. The steel ripped the flesh from his bones and blood poured from the wound down his chest. Tony had Chuck leaking, but that still didn't satisfy him. Harold came in immediately after and shut the door behind him.

"Yeah Blood, we know you been talking to the cops and Keem was trying to put that shit to rest. He just didn't finish the job. I heard you picked up some work from the Circle earlier, so where is it?" Harold walked up, smirked, and crashed his 9mm Berretta viciously upside Chuck's head causing an immediate knot as Chuck yelled, 'Aghhhh' and sunk deeper into the couch. He was on the loveseat and well out of range of his hand cannon. He was thinking that his life had reached its' expiration date, but he wished they would just go away.

Chuck knew eventually he would have to deal with these two clowns, but he didn't count on this. They came in the early morning and caught him slipping. *"Damn, these punk ass niggas 'bout to take me out,"* he thought as Tony yelled, "Where's it at muthafucka?"

The first shot filled the room as the .40 caliber slug ripped through Tony's neck, folding him like a poker hand. Harold tried to turn and fire, but met the first of the two slugs that would end his time on earth. The first bullet crashed into his lungs immediately and the second one ripped a hole in his heart. He spewed blood and let off one round into the floor as he fell backwards. Chuck didn't know what the fuck was going on in his apartment. He didn't know who was shooting, or where the shots were coming from. Each shot made him jump because he didn't know if they were headed in his direction. He had blood in his eyes and could only see blurry images, but he could hear very well. He heard Precious whisper in his ear with the sweetest voice he ever heard in his life, "Chuck, you okay baby?"

****

CeCe's heart was racing causing immense pain in her chest. The continuous flow of tears and snot traveled down from her eyes and nose as she cried her heart out. Her whole world had come crashing down when she heard her father murdered Brett, but the murder in Miami made her question the man she called Daddy.

"How could he do this to me?" CeCe sobbed loudly. She was barely able to speak. Erica rushed to her side; she was holding her and rocking her back and forth trying to console her. Erica's attempts were feeble and reality set in. CeCe came to grips with the fact that her father wasn't coming to get her.

All she could think about was how her father smiled and promised to come pick her up, and now he was in jail and denied bond. He always treated her like a queen, spoiled her and gave her the world. CeCe didn't know how she was going to make it without him. Only time would tell, since it looked like Vernon wasn't coming home soon. No matter how hard she cried and asked why, the answer was still the same. Her father, the only man who CeCe ever loved, was in jail for murder.

****

"Damn Baby, if you wouldn't have been here these clowns would've murked me," Chuck angrily said while glaring at the two dead men on the floor. "Ole punk ass muthafuckas," he hissed as he kicked their bodies.

"What we gon' do now?" Precious asked. She was making it clear that the police weren't about to be called this morning. She wasn't new to this shit, she was true to it. The shots went unnoticed to the world, and Blaze was out somewhere with a stem sizzling. There was no need for these bodies to go in for an autopsy. Chuck figured they would gather up the bodies and dump them in Winston Lake while the police were switching shifts. He knew he needed to weigh them down, so he decided to go outside to look for something to do that with. He found two pieces of concrete that each weighed at least eighty pounds and brought them back into the house. He used his new comforter, as well as his old one, and placed a body in each. After grabbing a knife from his room, he made Precious cringe when he sliced Harold from his chest to his waist. He stuffed the concrete block inside and smashed his intestines. He wanted to make sure the body sunk straight to the bottom of the lake. He repeated the same gruesome procedure with Tony, and wrapped each of them in a blanket and sealed them with duct tape.

Tony's El Camino sat in front of the apartment building. Chuck and Precious took the bodies and stuffed them in the back like they were loading a pickup truck. He put a sheet over the top of them in an attempt to conceal his human cargo. He changed his clothes and rinsed the blood off his hands and face and looked at himself in the mirror. His eyes were as cold as they were as a child, but his heart was much, much colder.

The two left the apartment and went to dump the bodies. They came back to grab something to eat at Bojangles. They both enjoyed steak, egg and cheese biscuits and Bo rounds to celebrate the fact that he severed the last ties that could link him to the T-Bone and Chico murder. It was finally over and he could rest a little easier.

****

Vernon was awakened from his sleep when the lights in the facility came on. He got up to eat the horrible breakfast of lumpy tasteless oatmeal, some kind of egg substitute, and a burned piece of toast. This morning, he was lucky to have the newspaper to read while he tried to eat. He couldn't believe his eyes when he saw his story on the front page. There was information in the story that even he was not privy to just yet. He was clueless to the murder in Miami, but the Hispanic name let him know that Caesar had to be responsible. *"Why the hell would he use the gun from a previous murder?"* he thought.

"White, you have an attorney visit," the officer called out to him as he opened the iron bars to escort him to a secure room reserved for attorney-client privilege.

Jackie was waiting in the room dressed in a black Brooks Brothers suit and sitting at the table. Vernon at 6' towered over Jackie Jones' 5'5" frame. Jackie had a round bald head, stocky frame, and a goatee. His skin looked bright red in color and he always wore his signature fedora. He was a pit bull in court and worked directly for Jesús.

"How you holding up?" Jackie stood to shake Vernon's hand before he sat down.

"I'm not good. I just read in the paper that I'm being extradited to Miami for another murder. I can't go down for this bullshit. I did confess to the one here, but damn, another one? That's some whole other shit," Vernon pushed away from the table and rose from his seat.

"Yeah, I just caught wind of that myself. I don't know what to say right now. I'm going to relay the facts to Jesús when I get back to Atlanta and see what he wants to do. This could play out in our favor. They'll try you for the murder here before you ever make it to Miami, so first things first. I'm going to have to see what I can do to get around your confession. It looks like I have my work cut out for me. Don't worry, one way or another, I'm going to get you out of this place. No murder is going to dampen our business relationship because we need you back. Sit tight, you may do a year just waiting to go to trial in this town," Jackie explained.

"A year?"

"You're facing a double homicide, a year is a cake walk compared to the time that could lie ahead of you. We may need a year to build our case."

Vernon sighed, but he knew his lawyer was telling the truth. He was in jail for murder and facing two life sentences. He knew he would never get two life sentences; after all he had been a loyal member in one of the biggest drug rings in the country. When he had his daughter at sixteen, he was just starting to peak in his career. As a consequence, he missed much of CeCe's young life.

Tonya Baxter, CeCe's mother, was just fifteen when she gave birth. She was the most beautiful woman that Vernon had ever laid eyes on. They met in the mid 70's during heroin's reign as the number one drug. He started as a small-time hustler selling nicks and dimes. His connects expanded quickly, and his profits did the same. With his new found wealth, he showered Tonya with gifts. He purchased her the house that he, his mother, and CeCe currently resided. He also ensured she and his daughter lived a lavish lifestyle. When he had free time, he would come home and spoil the two of them to death with trinkets.

Vernon had his operation extremely structured. He merely had to keep up with the amount of kilos that went out, and when and where they went. That was what caught the attention of Jesús. Once he was recruited to join the Dragon Cartel, he scheduled drop offs and pick-ups from Miami to New York. When his wife got sick, he was promoted to Distribution Manager. His new job title allowed him to work a bullshit job as a front, while he had millions in offshore accounts.

CeCe had no clue about any of her father's dealings in the drug game. Vernon wanted to shield her from that lifestyle. After Tonya's death, he knew that he was the only person his young daughter had left in the world. He also knew that he could have her well taken care of from inside these walls. He would never leave his baby girl completely alone. He gave Jackie the information to drop ten thousand dollars in her bank account. It would be a nice start for CeCe, enough to buy a car and have money for other expenses.

****

Erica finally gave in to CeCe's repeated requests to be taken home. She wanted to be alone and cry by herself. CeCe gazed out the window and had fleeting visions of what once was during the ride. She saw her mom, dad, and even herself. The more she reflected on her childhood, the more curious she became of her father and his whereabouts during much of that time.

He would always take her and her mom on extravagant trips and was always doing something fun with them. There were always times that Vernon wasn't around, but he would tell her, "Daddy gotta go make the donuts." She actually thought her father was a baker. To her, he was the nicest and sweetest man in the world. How do you go from being the nicest man in the world to an alleged murderer?

When Erica pulled up to her house, she looked at her friend with big red swollen eyes and a red nose to match. She managed to say, "Thank you, I really appreciate you." She and Erica hugged one another until CeCe tore away and reluctantly went inside the house. She dragged herself up the steps, into her room, and she crashed on the bed. She curled up in the fetal position and sucked her thumb like a toddler. Meanwhile, millions of sperm were swimming around her fallopian tubes looking for an egg to fertilize, and the HIV virus was starting to settle into her blood stream.

Chapter 15

Picking up the pieces definitely wasn't going to be easy. CeCe felt the pain every minute, second, and hour her father was away from her. She had been dodging his calls and she couldn't bring herself to go see him just yet. Going to school every day seemed more like a chore, but she managed to keep her grades up. She was determined to graduate and make it to college. Her mother instilled in her the importance of education at an early age. CeCe could still hear Tonya's voice, "*Go to college, graduate, find a good man, and then get married.*" It was as if her mother's words were etched in her brain.

CeCe spent most of her time in a fantasy world and she built a wall to shield her raw emotions. She wanted to appear strong to her friends, teachers and the students she came in contact with. There were no more after school activities; she attended school only to learn. She didn't waste time making new friends; she was fine with Erica and Destiny as her support group. She was content with spending a little time with Kevin. Kevin knew some shit, that's for sure. He taught her how to squirt; she only saw girls do that in the porno movies that they loved to watch. CeCe was gone off his tongue game, plus he was spending paper on her. Picking her up, taking her out, and licking her on command was his duty. It didn't matter where they were, she would bury his face into her freshly shaven pussy. She kept his face glossy like he wore lip gloss. She had virtually forgotten about Chuck.

Two weeks had passed and CeCe still hadn't met Kevin's parents. While they were at Olive Garden having dinner, CeCe popped the question on him.

"So, when am I gon' meet your parents?" She sat across from him at the table smiling from ear to ear as she gazed into his mesmerizing baby blue eyes.

"Well," he gulped, then reached for his water trying to stall for time. He took a sip and sat the glass down slowly, "CeCe. I have to be honest with you. I like you, I really do. We have fun together. My parents are not like me, and my grandfather was a founding KKK member in this county. I'm not proud of it, but it is what it is. They would never approve of me dating a black girl..." was the last thing CeCe heard, but Kevin's lips continued to move.

She was trying to process the information that she was just given, so she jumped in and cut him off, "So you're saying I can't meet your parents because I'm just some black pussy for you to fuck in the park, in the car, and anywhere else your dick gets hard?" She was starting to get hostile and the situation was getting ugly. The smile she wore earlier had packed up and went on vacation and she was looking for answers.

"CeCe calm down, no need to make a scene," Kevin spoke nervously, looking around to see if anybody was watching them.

"Now you don't want the black girl to get ghetto and make a scene in the restaurant. Let me calm the fuck down then," CeCe spoke clenching her teeth and slamming her fists onto the table. She was thoroughly pissed.

****

"That girl over there wild ain't she," Precious said to Chuck, but his mind was on his recent brush with death.

She and Chuck sat in a booth by the window at Olive Garden, but he couldn't get his mind off the fact that someone put Harold and Tony up to robbing him. He wanted that person dead. He was still fucking Precious, but she had been reaching too deep into his pockets since she saved his life. She took full advantage of the fact that she was Bonnie to his Clyde, but he wasn't feeling her in that way.

Yeah he liked Precious, and she did save his life, but that didn't mean that they had to get married. He felt like she was trying to take over his life. *"So what she's older than me, I don't need her. And hell, she aint do shit for me that I wouldn't have done for her ass. Why I gotta keep feeling like I owe this bitch?"* he thought while his eyes were fixed on a light outside the restaurant.

"Chuck, did you hear me?" Precious said with attitude.

"Huh," he snapped to, and dreaded the look she was giving him. He knew it meant she was about to piss him off.

"What the hell you looking at?" she spat.

"Tha fuck you mean? I'm looking outside. I heard yo ass. You telling me to look at some bitch tripping, like I really give a flying fuck. That's they business, damn." Chuck's forehead was wrinkled, and if his skin was transparent, she would've been able to see his blood boiling. He was absolutely tired of her and her shit.

"Who you talking to like that?" Precious said. She too was now heated.

"Man for real, let's just let this shit go."

"Nah, ain't no letting shit go. Obviously you got some shit you been wanting to say. So let's finish this conversation," Precious angrily said.

"Man, let's just chi…" Chuck started but was cut off.

"Nah, chill hell muthafucka, you don't talk to me like that lil boy. I'm a grown ass woman and I demand respect. Fuck you fa real fa real, and you can sit here and have this shit by your damn self. I'll call a ride." Precious jumped up, grabbed her coat and purse, then doused him with a glass full of cold water. The lemon clung to his shirt and the water dripped down his pants.

Precious turned around and stormed out of the restaurant. She didn't care that she was making a scene. Chuck sat and looked around at the other patrons, he was fuming. He wanted to run up, snatch her by her hair, and beat her ass in front of everybody. *You got charges and you don't need no more*," he told himself as he let her leave peacefully.

****

CeCe spotted Chuck from the corner of her eye and couldn't believe her luck. All she could think about was being with him in the shower and him busting off in her mouth. It didn't seem so bad now; in fact Kevin had her swallowing his kids like Vanessa Del Rio. He looked so sexy to her and something about him looked different. He had on a lime green and black Cross Colors shirt, black jeans, and a fresh pair of black BDP's, or Air Force Ones. He had two gold ropes hanging on his chest and a Jesus piece hanging from the hollow chain. His gold nugget watch looked like Wonder Woman's bracelet on one arm, and the other arm had a bracelet the same size as his watch. Chuck was getting his shine on.

She looked at Kevin and figured it was time to get him away from her. "You know what?" she asked giving him the evil look, "If you don't want me to cause a scene, I suggest you just get the fuck out of here. I'll call my grandmother to come and get me."

Kevin was perplexed; he wasn't sure how to react. However, he figured he would take her up on her offer. He didn't feel like taking her back home anyway, and he was tired of her showing out and embarrassing him. His black friends always told him horror stories about black women and how they sometimes go psycho. He took her advice and cut his losses; he got up and left CeCe alone.

****

The waitress returned and placed the plates on the table. Chuck was starving and about to punish the steak and shrimp he ordered. A bowl of chicken and shrimp alfredo was placed in front of him.

"Somebody sitting here?" CeCe's sweet voice tickled his ear.

"What you doing here?"

"Well, I'm here to eat," she felt his damp shirt, "I see you came from the water park," she giggled.

"I see you got jokes," he stood up and offered her the seat. "Here, sit down. The food just got here, and I'm dining alone."

CeCe slid in the booth, "Umm hmm, dining alone. I saw that girl throw her water at you."

"Oh you saw that, huh? I guess you don't think you caught my eye while you were over there with that white boy. That's your new boo?"

"Was she yours?" CeCe rolled her neck.

"Nah, I don't have a boo. I thought you were gon' be that, but you tried to play me at the game that night."

"Yeah," CeCe's facial expression softened, "I'm sorry about that. Then I was going to beep you, but all that stuff happened with my dad; I haven't been the same. I was lonely, and Kevin was just looking out for me."

"Yeah, I peeped that on the news that night after I saw you. You know the police questioned me for the same murder?"

CeCe put her head down.

"What's wrong?"

"I knew they were investigating you for that."

"What?"

"Yeah," she looked at his puzzled expression, and began to explain. She wanted to put the pieces together for him. "Remember that day we went to eat lunch at Burger King?

"Of course," Chuck replied.

"Well when we came back, the dude Brett saw us and he was the one who beat me and put me in the hospital."

"Word," he cut her off, "What he jump on you for?"

"Because we used to mess around."

"Used to mess around? Why didn't you tell me that?" Chuck began to get pissed all over again.

"There wasn't nothing really to tell, he wasn't my man."

"You know they jumped me after I dropped you off?"

"Huh?" her face immediately showed concern.

"Hell yeah, them clowns jumped me. I went looking for him when I left the hospital and stumbled on the murder scene. If your dad didn't get to him, I would have done it myself." Chuck spat lightly. He was careful to not make another scene. He had given the crowd enough entertainment for one night.

"Chuck I'm sorry, I didn't know," CeCe's eyes began to water again. She thought she was becoming more emotional lately, but she blamed it on stress.

"It's all good, no need to dwell on the past. That was yesterday, this is today ya feel me. Don't cry, dry your eyes and here comes your mother with those two little guys," Chuck imitated Slick Rick and Dougie Fresh's classic "Lodi Doddi" prompting CeCe to bust out laughing. They both were happy to be in each other's company and decided to enjoy the moment.

****

Precious sat outside in the parking lot watching Chuck. She saw him smiling and laughing it up with the same young bitch that was tripping earlier. She was thinking that he pissed her off on purpose and hoped she would leave.

"Oh word? This muthafucka gon' try to play me for some young bitch? That was his plan? To disrespect me and make me leave him so he could be with her? And she was with a white dude.   I see what kind of games this nigga trying to play. After I saved his punk ass, and helped him get rid of the bodies.   I got something for your ass muthafucka, watch."
Precious said to her friend as if she were talking to Chuck. She continued to hit the blunt as "Niggaz 4 Life" by NWA played in the background.

"You ready to go?" he asked her. He was tired of sitting there watching Chuck.

"Yeah let's get up out of here. We gon' see his ass later. Revenge is a dish best served cold," Precious said with a smirk on her face that could kill.

****

"Ahhh man," Chuck laughed as they continued to talk after they devoured their food. CeCe was so hungry she smashed Precious' food as if she had ordered it off the menu herself.

"Yeah, those were the times," CeCe capped off the old school convo about how her and her friends used to get into mischief. She hadn't laughed and smiled this much since their first date. Chuck was really special and she figured out quickly that she had been sleeping on him. His smile still had the same effect on her; he was still giving her wet the panty syndrome.

Chuck paid the bill then asked, "So you coming wit' me?"

"Where we going?"

"It's Friday and it's a party at the Convention Center tonight. We can get some drinks and hit that joint up."

"I don't wanna go dressed like this, and I don't wanna go home. My grandma's been getting on my nerves."

Chuck looked at his watch, "Well it's only eight and the mall doesn't close till nine."

"So what you saying? You gon' buy me something to wear?" CeCe smiled.

"Of course, you can't roll with me and not be fly too," Chuck smiled and got up so they could leave and hit the mall.

When they walked outside, CeCe looked around for his car as she scanned the parking lot. She didn't see it so she asked, "Where you parked at?"

"Right there," he pointed the key fob and pressed the button. The horn and lights chirped on a gleaming cherry red BMW.

"Oh shit! That's tight," CeCe admired the brand new four-door 1992 BMW 525i. The car's new sleek design made her panties wet again and confirmed her suspicions that Chuck had bread.

"Yeah, I just got this like two days ago," Chuck responded as he opened her door.

CeCe sat her round ass on the butter soft leather seats and stroked her finger across the wood grain on the dash. She was taking in all the luxury. This ride was like a dream car. Chuck shut the door and walked around to climb into the driver's seat.

When he turned the key, the dashboard lit up a bright orange color and the bass dropped for Slick Rick's "Children's Story." They both bobbed their heads in unison. Olive Garden was in the Hanes Mall parking lot, so they only drove around to the front of the new mall. The mall was packed as usual, a lot of kids their age hung out here on Friday nights.

The two exited the car and headed for the entrance. Chuck grabbed CeCe's hand and smiled at her, she smiled and turned to him and kissed him on the cheek. She loved when money was being spent on her. Her father had her spoiled rotten and she expected any guy she dated to break bread.

Chuck didn't care; he had been getting more and more money since he linked up with Will-G. His spot was booming and the cash was pouring in. He had a non-stop crack spot. There were never fiends outside hanging around waiting to get high either. Blaze kept the party going down in his crib, so there was no need to for them to hang outside and make the spot hot.

CeCe picked out a black Guess acid wash jean outfit with tight fitting pants that had holes in them, and white leggings to wear underneath. The leggings matched the words on her shirt and coordinated with her shell toe black and white Adidas. CeCe loved the B-Girl look, and it looked great on her. She had just gotten her hair done in fresh finger waves, so she was making sure she was gon' be seen.

Chuck decided on a L.A. Raiders sweat shirt, a pair of black Levis, and a pair of Adidas that matched CeCe's. He found a black Raiders snap back cap to top off the sweat shirt. They were going to be fly tonight and Chuck knew once he got her back to his crib after the party, it was gon' be on. He missed that good pussy, and he was definitely trying to get some of that again tonight. He didn't get a chance to represent like he wanted the last time, so she was definitely in for it tonight.

Chapter 16

Chuck and CeCe headed back to his crib to get dressed for the party. They pulled up in front of his building, he turned off the lights, and they went inside to take a quick shower and change.

Chuck let CeCe get in the shower first while he took care of his business. He secretly rented the apartment across the hall from his and started stashing his money and drugs there. He only went inside when nobody was around, so he was the only person who knew about the apartment. The unit underneath was empty, so he had no concerns about someone hearing footsteps.

He grabbed a Big Eight, or four and a half ounces of cocaine from the kilo that he had stashed in the bedroom. He then locked the safe that he had bolted to the closet floor. He never turned the lights on when he went inside; he could see well enough in the dark to maneuver. He went back to his apartment and replenished his "Coke on Deck" box. He never told anybody where his money or drugs were, but he always had a dummy stash that he worked from in the apartment. It was a few grams short of one hundred and twenty-five. In case he got caught with it, he would only catch three years of state time. Chuck knew the game and said fuck doing twenty years Fed time for having everything in one place.

Just as he shut the closet door, CeCe came prancing out smelling like a fresh summer breeze. She was making his dick stiff, but he wanted to get in the shower so they could get down to the party. His peoples Jimmy from the south side wanted to buy the Big Eight. Chuck usually didn't sell weight, but since he was working with at least 1000 Grams at a time he figured he could sell a few ounces wholesale. He only dealt weight to a few dudes that he knew. There were too many cats getting popped and snitching trying to save their asses. Chuck wasn't going out like that.

****

Precious sat outside in the car waiting for Chuck and CeCe to leave. She still couldn't believe Chuck was playing her like this.

"Muthafuckas don't believe shit stank, until they can smell it," she growled. He couldn't have been thinking clearly at the restaurant, in her mind. Bobby Digital, her partner who came to pick her up from the Olive Garden, sat on the passenger side of the all black Toyota Wagon. It was kitted up with the windows tinted and some chrome five star wheels. The license plate read: Buggin. Everybody and their momma knew he was the one driving the car.

"So what's good? We gon' go in there and kill these muthafuckas or what?" Bobby's gold fronts glistened and the mouthpiece made him talk like he had a lisp.

Precious didn't want to murder Chuck, so she thought long and hard about answering that question. Bobby was a loose cannon; he was always down for whatever. She knew she had to be specific on how she wanted things to play out. His trigger finger was always itching. Imported straight from the mean streets of Brooklyn, Bobby Digital was the epitome of a menace to society. He was two hundred and twenty six pounds of mostly fat, and 5"10" tall. He had skills with his hands and loved to box with dudes. Usually he would knock 'em out and then kill 'em.

"No, we gon' wait till he leave, then go in and rob his ass. It's not time for him to die yet, we still need him. We just gon' take what he got right now and when he go re-up, we gon' get him and his connect and kill them both. Never kill for nothing Bobby," Precious looked at him, "Murder cases cost a lot of cash, if you catch one. You have to make sure you don't leave any witnesses or evidence."

****

Chuck got a page from Jimmy that said he didn't have all the money at the moment, so he decided to holla at him after the party. He and CeCe were looking good in their matching black and white outfits.

"You look good boo," Chuck told her while she was taking one last look at her breasts sitting nicely in her lace bra.

"Thanks, you ready to go?"

"Yeah, let's get out of here," Chuck instructed as he tucked the .45 in his waist band.

CeCe looked at him tuck the gun away and didn't really know how to feel about it. Winston-Salem had gotten crazy, and his friend did try to kill him. She figured he was only paranoid. She knew what kind of life he was into and that he would rather get caught with it than without it.

The two left the apartment and Chuck locked the dead bolt and the bottom lock. They went and got into the car and he decided to ride down to the circle to turn around. He was really trying to get a better look at the black wagon parked 2 spaces from him. The car raised his interest; he knew who the driver was when he saw the license plate. He couldn't see anything inside the car and wondered why it was sitting there.

****

"Damn, I wonder if he saw us," Precious looked up, watching the tail lights disappear up the street.

"Nah, if he woulda seen us we woulda been in a gunfight by now."

"Good, well come on and let's go on up in here," Precious opened the door, "Come on!"

"I'm coming, damn you always so pushy."

They got out and crept inside the apartment building and made their way upstairs. Bobby kicked the door open and the two of them searched the apartment looking for drugs and money. They were only able to find the Big Eight that Chuck had left in the closet. They also found $5,000 in the top right hand dresser drawer; this was only his pocket money and he always kept some there. The duo was satisfied with the small score and thought that they were really doing something. Little did they know, the real money and drugs were across the hall. They ran back to the car and hopped in to flee the scene.

"We got a big bag of coke and a wad of money, shit I'm good with half of all that," Bobby said while pulling off. Precious examined the bag and knew they had to miss something.

****

CeCe strolled into the party at the Convention Center and the music was rocking. They were playing "Planet Rock" as she stepped through the door and the dance floor was packed. Everybody was jamming and she was ready to rush in and get her groove on.

The place was packed, everybody was all smiles and having a good time. When she rushed to the floor, she saw two familiar faces on the dance floor getting it in. She walked up behind Erica and tapped her on the shoulder.

"Uh huh bitch, you didn't even tell me you were going to be up in here," CeCe yelled over the music.

"Heyyyy girl!" Erica reached out to embrace her friend in a hug. "What you doing here? Who you with?"

"I drove my friend Chuck's car, but he should be coming in a little bit. He said he had some business to handle and he was going to catch a ride down here."

"Who is Chuck?" Destiny cut in, "What happened to Kevin?"

"It's a long story, I'll tell you later. Let's jam," CeCe screamed when Breed and 2pac's "Gotta Get Mine" began to pound through the speakers. The trio all started to dance, smile, and have a good time.

****

Chuck glanced up to check their location and noticed that they were sitting at the stop light on Third St. and MLK Blvd. He listened to the conversation go back and forth as he began to pull the pistol from his side. He aimed at the driver's head first.

"Hey, I'm hungry you tryin..." Bobby spoke, before the sound of gunfire filled the air and his brain exploded onto the windshield. Before Precious could scream or turn around, her skull was split and brain fragments were splattered on the passenger side windshield.

Chuck climbed from the hatchback; he had crept in the back while they were robbing his house. Reaching in Precious' lap, he grabbed the bag with his money and drugs. He opened the door, still wearing the latex gloves, and hopped out of the back seat. He calmly headed towards the Exxon gas station to call a cab and go to the party.

****

Chuck tipped the cab driver to take him back to his crib first so he could drop the bag off. He looked at the door that was damaged and went downstairs to bang on Blaze's door. Finally, he was able to wake him up. Blaze opened the door looking like stir fried shit.

"What's up Young Blood," Blaze wiped his eyes.

"Yo, somebody kicked in my door earlier!"

"What? Who?"

"It don't matter. Just go fix my door so it'll shut and have it done before I get back from this party. I got a broad with me, so I don't want her to know what happened."

"Aight, I got you," Blaze answered as Chuck left.

He arrived at the party and exited the cab. He was ready to go inside and get his party on. He wasn't concerned that the police cars racing downtown were on their way to a murder scene he left behind. He sprinkled some powder in the car to make the case drug related.

When Chuck finally walked inside, the DJ was playing LL Cool J's "I Need Love." CeCe was easy to spot standing with the white girl and the skinny black chick. He walked up from behind and tapped her on the shoulder.

"Wanna dance?

CeCe was startled at first, but Chuck's smile made her feel comfortable. "Sure, why not?" she smiled back.

Chuck took her hand and they began weaving through the crowd to find a spot in the middle of the dance floor. He drew her in close, closed his eyes, and swayed side to side to the beat. The closeness of their bodies conjured up emotions that were building between them.

Their hearts seemed to beat perfectly as her chest was pressed up against his. When LL went off, Keith Sweat's "Make It Last Forever" came on. The beat was more up tempo, but they still danced and smiled at each other. It was like they were falling in love. Even though the place was crowded, in their minds the two of them were the only two people in the room. They were lost in each other's eyes and the mood seemed so right.

"Come on Baby, let's get out of here. Let's go have our own party." Chuck whispered with his forehead resting on hers.

"Ok, let's go," CeCe panted. She was as horny as she had ever been.

****

The soulful sounds of the Quiet Storm bounced off the wall as Chuck spread baby oil over CeCe's back. Luther Vandross' "If This World Were Mine" played softly in the background. His hands moved seductively against her skin; CeCe had never felt a touch so soft and sensual. Chuck was taking his time and he was going to give her a night she would always remember. He flipped her over on her back and wasted no time diving face first in between her legs. He began to suck on her clit sending sensations through her body that she had never experienced, not even with Kevin. "Ummmmm," she moaned as he licked and sucked her body into convulsions. "Ohhhh Chuck!" she screamed.

Chuck knew that she was caught in his spell as he removed his face from between her legs. He didn't wait for any head; he was ready to dive in. He penetrated her softly, going deep into her inner depths as she grabbed a hold of his back. He methodically moved in and out, swirling his dick around while bouncing off her walls and ultimately hitting the bottom. "Oh Baby, fuck me," CeCe said in his ear taking him fully inside her. She was taking that entire dick like a champ.

CeCe was huffing and puffing and moaning and groaning as he gave her the dick slowly. She felt every inch of him and his sex was mind blowing. She was cumming back to back and her legs wouldn't stop shaking. Chuck was bringing tears to her eyes. He was laying the pipe unlike any other dude that she fucked with.

CeCe's pussy was super wet, and it made him cum without warning. He kept stroking though and their juices just mixed in and dripped from her to the bed.

Chuck flipped her around like a ragdoll. He dicked her from the back, the side, on her belly, pulled her hair, smacked her ass, choked her, and even got caught up in digging her out and called her a bitch. She loved every minute of it; she was a true freak. He made her feel so good that she was finally sure that she wanted to be with him and was ready to let Kevin and her old Sugar Daddies go. His dick rung bells in her eardrums and made her drip excessively.

They went at it for two hours, both reaching numerous orgasms before they fell off and lay beside each other. She felt safe with him and for some odd reason she felt whole again. He was everything she wanted and needed. Tonight made it official for the both of them. Chuck and CeCe were officially an item. They washed each other off and drifted into a deep sleep together.

****

Chuck woke up with CeCe laying on his chest still in a deep sleep. He landed a soft kiss on her forehead which prompted her to open her eyes.

"Good morning," she spoke. She was careful not to blow her breath in his face; her morning breath was fierce.

"Good morning, how did you sleep?"

"Not to well. I've been thinking about my dad a lot."

"You haven't been to see him yet?"

"No, I was mad at him."

"So why don't you go today? I'll take you down there."

"I don't know. I'm still upset that he left me. He was all I had out here, now I feel like a black girl lost. He's not going to be around for the holidays, and he's going to miss my birthday and Valentine's Day."

"You gon' have to get over your feelings. Your father needs you. Next week is Thanksgiving and I'm sure he would love to see you. You're obviously the most important thing in his life."

"How could that be true? He left me. Now that I've been thinking back to my childhood, he was always missing. He always said he was making donuts, but ain't no telling what he was up to."

"Why you say that?"

"How many parents you know turn into a killer overnight?"

"I don't know, I guess you're right. How could you even find out?"

CeCe shrugged, "I don't know, but I'm looking for answers. I want to know who Vernon White really is. It's like I don't know him anymore."

"Have you talked to him at all?"

"No, and I don't want to right now."

"CeCe tomorrow is not promised to any of us. We have to try and live our days as best we can, and love those we have while they are still here. Even if you don't go tonight, make sure you go on Thanksgiving. He already gotta eat that bullshit food. At least make his day with your beautiful smile."

A knock at the door interrupted their conversation and Chuck got up to see who was on the other side. It was a sale and another came right after that one, and then another. Eventually, he had to let CeCe see what was going down. He ran out of rocks, so he had to cook up another ounce. This wasn't the love shack, this was the trap house. There was money to be made rain, hail, sleet or snow.

CeCe had never been around drugs before and almost gagged at the smell of the cocaine cooking on the stove. She was fascinated to see him cooking crack and chopping it down to pieces for sale. He showed her what twenties were and even let her start making sales so she could get accustomed to the process of making easy money. She caught on quickly; she loved the thrill and relative ease.

Chuck got a kick out of watching CeCe slang pieces and collect money. He virtually turned her into a drug dealer in record time. He found it sexy that she wanted to be a hustler. He figured the more he taught her, the more valuable she would become. He was happy with her being around the house and decided that he wanted her to stay with him for a while.

"So CeCe, what would you say if I wanted you to say here with me?"

"Well," she was caught completely off guard, "I wouldn't mind staying here. I'm tired of my grandma, and it's time for me to get out on my own and get my grown woman on. What about the girl I saw you with at Olive Garden?"

"What about her?"

"Ain't she your boo?"

"Nah, you my boo."

"I don't want any drama Chuck, she seems crazy. She threw water all over you," CeCe laughed.

Chuck gritted his teeth, hating the fact that she was laughing at him.

"That's not funny," he spat.

"Awwww baby," she climbed up under him to hug him, "I'm just playing."

"Yeah, yeah, yeah, anyway that chick was nobody and you won't see her anymore. She's gone."

"Good, then we can focus on us. I have to go get my clothes; I guess I'll use the other bedroom to store my stuff."

"Yeah that'll work. I can take you to go get your things later. You need to go see your dad though for real."

"I'll go on Thanksgiving, just like you said."

Chapter 17

"Urrggghhh," CeCe bent over in the toilet spewing her guts out. The smell of toilet water was no help and the nausea was eating away at the lining of her stomach. She spit up her meal of burgers and fries from last night and now she was spitting yellow stomach acid.

"You ok baby?" Chuck asked watching her on bended knees.

"No," CeCe coughed into the toilet holding onto the seat for dear life. She desperately wanted the sickness to go away. This was not the way she planned to start off Thanksgiving. She was nervous about her upcoming visit with her father. She had been feeling sick since their sex session the previous night.

"You need me to get you something?"

"A ginger ale would be great."

Chuck shook his head thinking, *"Why the hell everybody always thinks ginger ale is the remedy for everything. The way they look at ginger ale in the south, you would think it was a magic potion."*

"Okay baby, I'll be right back," he said and left to go to the BP to grab a soda.

CeCe finished up in the bathroom and flushed her mess. She pulled up on the sink and leaned towards the faucet. She started shoveling water in her mouth trying to elimate the stale taste. She looked at herself in the bathroom mirror and spoke, "CeCe, I hope you ain't fucked up girl. You missed your period by a week, and you have been feeling sick. Please don't let this be happening, what am I gon' do?" she watched her lips move but her reflection didn't have an answer. She was going to have to make a doctor's appointment. She finished up in the bathroom and went back in the bedroom to lay down. She looked up at the ceiling and thought to herself:

> *"Damn, I think I done fucked up. What am I gon' do? I don't have nobody to talk to and I'm tired of crying. I have never shed this many tears, I'm tired of this shit. I have to lift my head up and grow up. I done left home and got a good man. I have to learn how to be a grown woman. If we about to have a baby, then we gon' make this thing work. My mom had me when she was young, if she could do it, I can too,"* she thought.

Who was she kidding? Burying emotions is not the best way to deal with life, but it's what she chose to do. Now she was trying to figure out how she was going to tell her father that she might be pregnant…again.

****

"Damn, who is that?" Chuck said over the music pumping through the Alpine system as he backed into a spot at BP.

She had on a pair of bedroom shoes, jogging pants, and a black leather jacket zipped all the way up with a pajama shirt hanging out the bottom. Even with her hair under a toboggan, she looked good. No makeup or fancy clothes covered Brenda Collins as she left the house to run to the store to grab some milk for her macaroni and cheese.

Chuck put his car in park and hopped out with his swag turned all the way up. Even though he was just going to the store, he still had on his outfit from last night. His gold was shining on the thick Gucci link and herring bone chain he wore. The link hung lower than the herring bone and the Uzi charm sat right above his navel. He wasn't the average dope boy, he was getting serious money.

Chuck went to the freezer to grab a Canada Dry ginger ale and walked up behind Brenda's big ole booty, "Hey, how you doing?" he smiled.

"Hey, I'm fine and you?" she looked at this sexy ass dude smiling down on her.

"I'm good, Happy Thanksgiving."

"Well Happy Thanksgiving to you too."

"$3.61 is your change," the African male behind the counter interrupted the connection between the two.

Brenda reached for her change, smiled and said, "Thank you" to the store clerk. She started to walk out when a strong hand grabbed her arm gently.

"Wait, let me walk you outside," Chuck asked her as the clerk rung up his soda.

She started to reject his offer, but it was something about the $5000 wad of cash he dug out of his pocket to give the clerk a dollar for the soda. Money talked and it was telling her to see what this dude was about. Not only was he fine as hell, but he was paid. She was seeking a sponsor because her man was recently sentenced to ten years in the state penitentiary. She figured maybe she could get this dude for some of his money and hopefully get some good dick out of the deal too.

"So what's your name?" Chuck asked as he held the door open for her.

"Brenda, and yours?"

"C-Roy," he replied-giving himself a new nick name. He couldn't have random chicks running around saying, "I fucked Chuck."

"C-Roy? What kind of name is that? What's your real name?"

He beeped the alarm on his ride, "Charles, but I don't like that name. Please, just call me C-Roy," he looked into Brenda's deep brown eyes and he could have sworn that she looked like MC Lyte, but her body looked ten times better. Her ass was bouncing in her jogging pants and he assumed by the way her coat protruded from her chest, that her titties were big enough to bury his face in.

"Damn C-Roy, you doing the damn thing ain't you?" she said admiring his car.

"Yeah I do alright, I can't complain. Where's your car?" he looked around at the deserted parking lot.

"I walked up here. I live in South Gate. Why, you wanna drop me off at home?" she flashed all thirty two pearly whites.

"Yeah, come on," he answered smiling back, stepping inside his baby. He knew at this point that he was most definitely gon' hit that.

****

"Damn, where he go to get a damn soda?" CeCe said as she lay in bed.

She was still lost in her thoughts and all she could think about was going to see her father. What would his eyes look like gazing at her now? *"I wonder what kind of donuts he was making when he was away from me and mom,"* CeCe thought, but she was interrupted when Chuck walked in the house.

He came in smiling with the ginger ale, "Look what I got you baby!" he said smiling and smelling like a pound of weed.

"For real Chuck? You gon' take damn near an hour to go get me a soda from up the street and waltz in here like you ain't done shit? Then on top of that you smell like weed. Where the fuck you been?" CeCe's words flew from her mouth. If there were a voice pattern for 'Bitchy' her vocal cords epitomized it right now. Her tongue was mighty, and she was fed up. Not so much with Chuck, but men lying to her period. Her dad had been one big ass liar and she wanted to hear what kind of excuse was about to come from Chuck's lips.

"I been to the muthafuckin store and so what if I was riding and smoking. I went out to get something for yo ass and went and handled some business of my own. When the fuck did the world start revolving around you? I didn't get the memo," Chuck growled. His face screamed, "Bitch you better shut the fuck up talking to me right now."

CeCe belted out her mouth, "Who the fuck," she started, but her words were slapped into the form of spit and splattered on the headboard. That didn't go like she had planned it, and her face stung like Mike Tyson had just punched her. She reached up and grabbed her face with eyes full of tears. She refused to cry, but whimpered, "Nigga you gon' put your hands on me?"

"Bitch, you don't talk crazy to me! This is my muthafuckin house and you will respect me. I pay the cost to be the boss around this bitch, and you ain't bout to be talking to me like that," Chuck spat. He paced the floor telling CeCe to shut the fuck up and let him calm down.

She took the advice and said, "I'm about to get in the shower. I'm going to see my dad in a little bit and I hope and pray that your hand print is gone by then."

"And if it's not, bitch? Then what? Your daddy can't break out of jail and come get me and if he could-trust me this ain't what he want. I aint no sucka duck ass nigga, baleeve that!"

CeCe could not believe the words coming out of his mouth, and the tone of his voice stabbed her over and over shooting pain throughout her body. She had never been spoken to like that except the day when Brett slapped her down. Here she was again with the same one who sat by her side consoling her. He just slapped the shit out of her and was now cursing her out like a dog. This couldn't be her life. It felt like déjà vu. Another baby and another psycho, she couldn't believe her luck. "*Lord, please don't let me be pregnant by this man,*" she thought.

****

CeCe's face went back to normal by the time Chuck was taking her downtown. She really didn't have much to say to him, but he did apologize anyway. She understood they both had been under stress and he sounded genuine with his delivery.

Her mind was racing faster than the houses flying past as they made their way downtown. Chuck pulled up in front of the door and turned to CeCe, "I'll be back to get you. You have the car phone number right?"

"Yeah Baby, I got it. I'll give you a call when I'm ready," she told him, as she got out to go visit with her father.

The visitor's room was packed and she had to stand in line to sign in to see him. When she looked down the list, she saw a lady's name, Veronica Green. She had never heard that name before, so that raised her curiosity. "*He is so secretive,*" she said to herself before she took a seat to wait. She looked around the room and saw babies waiting to see their fathers everywhere. It almost reminded her of a daycare, but this was a much sadder version.

"*Why do dudes get themselves into trouble and have to see their kids in jail?*" she asked herself judging the guys on the inside. She then thought about that fact that her father was in there right along with them. "*Why did he do something so foolish? What was he thinking? Did he ever think about me and what I wanted?*" all these questions were running through her mind.

At last, it was finally time for her to be ushered back to a room with separated pieces of glass and phones on both sides for the inmates to communicate with the visitors. She sat waiting, still thinking of what questions to ask and what she was going to say. Her stomach was doing backflips and the man that was placed in front of her wasn't the same man that had dropped her off at school that day. His beard was full, his hair was growing into an afro, and he looked like something from the wild. The softness in his eyes was a distant memory and something about them said killer. Yet his demeanor had a pleasant tone.

They picked up the phones, "Happy Thanksgiving CeCe," her father's voice sung in her ear. She knew it was him once she heard his familiar voice.

"Happy Turkey Day Daddy! How you holding up in here? You don't really look like yourself."

"I'm not doing too good. I never wanted to be helpless and on this side of the window. Not being able to touch my baby girl and I'm going to miss that good food. What is your grandma cooking?"

CeCe shrugged.

"What do you mean?"

"I haven't really talked to Grandma," she held her glare. It was time for her to grow up and put her foot down.

"Huh? What does that mean?" he asked.

"It means that I haven't been staying there, I've been staying with Chuck."

Her words started twisting his stomach into knots, "What!"

"That's right. You left me alone, what was I supposed to do? You know I don't get along with her like that."

"CeCe honey," Vernon tried to remain calm, "You have to go to school and…"

"I do go to school Daddy. What, you think 'cause you threw your life away, I'm gon' do the same thing?" CeCe cut her father off. She was looking for a reaction, but his gaze remained cold-killer type cold.

"CeCe, baby, I know that you're upset. I know that I lied."

"Oh really? I'm glad you're telling the truth now. Why? Why did you do it?"

He sighed, and figured he would try to explain, "Baby Girl, you are all I have. I never put my hands on your mother, or even raised my voice at her. I always treated the two of you like the black queens that you are. I tried to do everything in my power to show you what a real man is and how you deserve to be treated."

"Yeah, I see how real men kill kids. Daddy you're a grown man in jail for killing a teenager. If I would have known you were going to do that, then I would have just pressed charges. He didn't deserve to die because he made a mistake. He could've apologized, but now he's gone. There's no coming back from death. How you think that makes me feel?"

Vernon felt small; here his daughter was teaching him how to be a man. She didn't know his hands were covered in more blood than just Brett's. She didn't know that her father had been, and was still, a member of a drug ring that stretched from Miami to California. He hid that part of his life from his daughter very well. He figured it was still no need to tell her now.

"I'm sorry. No matter how much I say it, you're not gon' accept my apology. So listen," he decided to get to business, "I had my lawyer set up an account for you. I put $10,000 in it and the card should be at your grandmother's house waiting for you. I need you to go and buy yourself a car. I want you to build up your credit score since you are getting older, so get a car that you have to make payments on in your name. The payments will be paid, don't worry about that part. Next, I want you to find a house in a nice neighborhood and rent it. I don't want you staying with no boys. Get your own. Get a list of all your monthly bills and send that information to my lawyer. Everything will be taken care of. I'm going to make sure you stay independent and I'm going to make your life comfortable so you can graduate. I'll be getting out of here in August, so until then I'm going to take care of your from here. I'm never going to leave you," he placed his hand on the window.

CeCe couldn't believe her ears, but she loved everything he said. She placed her small hands up against her father's palm and answered, "I love you Daddy. Are you really getting out of here?"

"Yes, and I'll tell you everything I never told you then. When you graduate we can move to whatever city you want to move too."

"Seriously Daddy!" Her heart was fluttering with excitement, "Oh my God I can't wait!"

Vernon was happy to see his daughter smile again. He knew he had to keep her from becoming dependent on a young man. If he couldn't be around to take care of her, his money could. Next year Winston-Salem could kiss him and his daughter goodbye. Even though a life had been taken, Vernon would never serve the time. Jesús would make sure of that.

Chapter 18

The phone was ringing inside the car, but Chuck and Brenda were engaged in deep conversation. He was learning what she was about and made a few coke sales while he sat in her hood. South Gate was just as hood as any other set of projects in Winston. Petty dealers roamed around looking for crack sales and crack heads combed the streets looking for the best crack.

Chuck had the best shit on that side of town, but he wasn't trying to take food off tables. He was making powder sales through Brenda, or B-Girl, as he liked to call her. With her help, he was gaining new customers. She was in the car looking scrumptious with her lip gloss poppin' and her sexy dick sucking lips glistened when she smiled. The two gold teeth in her mouth gave her a different sex appeal. She was like a sexy gangster girl, with a hood twist. She turned Chuck on.

B-Girl talked and smiled, but all the while sizing Chuck up. The big bag of powder he had with him was calling her name. She hadn't let the cat out the bag just yet, but she was getting around to it.

"So C-Roy, who was that?" B-Girl asked to see if he was gon' lie.

"Aint no telling, probably a sale. I'm busy talking to you though," he smiled.

"Awwww, what a gentlemen," B-Girl batted her eyes setting him up for the kill, "so you gon' let me get some of that stuff?"

"Hell yeah," Chuck cockily said, grabbing his meat to show her what he was working with.

"Umm, I see you packing, but I'm not talking 'bout the dick baby. I'm talking bout the powder."

"What you gon' do, sell it?"

"No silly, I'm gon' snort it!"

"You snort powder?" Chuck asked with his eyebrows raised. He always pictured coke in the same boat as crack, so he didn't think her sexy ass would be doing something like that.

"Yeah, don't you?"

"Nah, I never fucked with it. I always thought it was like crack."

"No silly, crack is for them broke muthafuckas who need a cheap hit. Cocaine is that bitch that cost and the broke need not apply."

"What does it do to you?"

"Let's do this, how bout we run and get some beer and cigarettes and I call up my girl Princess to swoop through. We can have a party for Thanksgiving. You got some liquor?"

"Yeah I got a fifth of Absolut at the crib. I don't stay too far from here, you trying to ride with me to go get it?"

"Yeah, let me go lock my door," B-Girl said then hopped out the car. The way her ass moved was a sight to behold. It bounced left and right and shook like a bowl of jello. Her hips swayed gracefully as his eyes undressed her. On her way back those fat ass thighs were screaming at Chuck, telling him he needed to dive in later. Not one time did CeCe cross his mind.

****

"Shit," CeCe barked at the phone. She was heated as she slammed the receiver down. She was beyond pissed that she depended on Chuck and he wasn't even answering the phone. "That's alright, I'm gon' to be ghost when I get my car next week, fareal," she snapped at the air, with no one listening. She wasn't going to let him ruin her Thanksgiving, so she dialed up a number she was sure to get an answer from.

"Hello?"

"Hey Grandma," CeCe spoke into the phone.

"Hey Baby! Where you at? The family's all here and we're about to eat soon. Your Aunt Chevella is looking for you."

"Ooooo Chevella is here? Yes! I'm downtown, I just went to see dad."

"That's good, how is he doing?"

"He's good, hey Grandma I need a ride from downtown. Can you ask Chevella to come and get me?"

"Yeah I'll send her; she should be there shortly."

CeCe hung up happier than she was when she picked up the phone. She hadn't seen her Aunt Chevella in forever. She was her mother's older sister, and was always the coolest. She used to come down a lot when CeCe was younger, but she hadn't been to Winston in a few years. When the black 1990 Mercedes pulled up, she was all smiles.

"Hey Auntie." CeCe hopped in the car excited and leaped to hug her before she even shut the door.

"Hey CeCe!" Chevella spoke as she hugged and kissed her niece.

"Where have you been girlfriend?" CeCe asked using the line they always used.

"Girlfriend, I've been super busy. You know I have a boutique I have to run and I'm getting close to opening up my own salon soon, so I stay busy."

"Oh for real girlfriend? That's what's up!"

CeCe always admired her Auntie who looked like she could be mixed with Asian the by the way her eyes slanted. Her smooth coco brown complexion made it obvious that she was indeed black. Her lips were curvy and sensual and her round cheeks displayed pits when she smiled. Her hair was long and straight hanging down her back, and it was silky and fine. Her eyebrows stayed arched, as well as her hands manicured and feet pedicured. She always wore heels; never would you catch her in a pair of sneakers.

"So Auntie you heard what happened to my dad?"

"Sort of, but I don't really care. We have to get him out of there. We are working on that right now."

"How can you say you don't care? And who is we?"

Chevella studied CeCe's face and searched for the right words, "Sweetheart, your father is a very powerful and rich man. He's not who you think he is."

"What's that mean? And we're not rich to me, why don't we live in a mansion?"

"Because your father is not flamboyant and he wanted his life here to seem normal."

CeCe was really confused now. What the hell was her Auntie talking about? She didn't understand anything at this point. Her father was now Mr. Mystery Man and Chevella wasn't making it any better.

As they were passing BP, she saw what looked like Chuck's car pulling in. She was on fire inside.

"Auntie, I need to go to that BP and get something, make a right here," she pointed at the next turn. They made a right, then another right on the next street, and were back at the BP. As they pulled in her suspicions were confirmed, it was him.

****

"You want something out the store?" Chuck asked B-Girl.

"Nah, just the beer and cigarettes."

Chuck opened the door and all the blood drained from his face. His ear drums filled quickly with "Oh for real muthafucka, you gon' leave me stranded for some bitch?" CeCe spat as she walked towards the car.

That one bitch was all it took for B-Girl to hop out the passenger seat, "Well what then bitch! I got your bitch right here."

"Hold up, hold up," Chuck jumped out to push CeCe back and his cheek warmed up from her soft hands. She slapped his ass mostly as payback from earlier.

"CeCe!" Chevella grabbed the .380 out of her purse and as Chuck drew his hand back a shot filled the air, "BANG!"

B-Girl backed up and Chuck jumped looking at the barrel of the gun approaching him. He thought he was tripping, but he knew from her look that she wasn't playing.

"You better back the hell away from my niece and put yo hand down. You not bout to put your hands on her and you better hop your ass back in the car lil girl," Chevella belted at B-Girl. She quickly obliged and got back in the car.

"How you gon' play me like this," CeCe went against the grain and the tears began to flow, even though she said she was done crying.

"Come on here CeCe," her Auntie tugged at her shirt, "You can handle this some other time. Let's go!"

CeCe did as she was told and she and Chevella hopped back in the Benz and peeled out.

"CeCe what was that shit all about?"

"I don't want to talk about it right now," CeCe continued to let tears fall and gazed out the window.

****

"Who the fuck was that bitch?"

"Man I'm goin' to get the beer," Chuck blew off the question and went in to get a case of Icehouse. "This bitch not 'bout to stress me out," he spoke out loud to himself. He paid for his stuff and went back to the car knowing Brenda was about to trip. He was wrong about that notion, because a dollar bill was hovering under her nose as she shoveled powder up her nostrils. "You gotta do that here?"

"Why not?" she sniffed wiping the residue from the tip of her nose, "I don't care about these people."

"If you don't care, I don't care," he shrugged and turned up "Dope man" by NWA as the bass dropped and they headed back to her house.

"Pull by that car right there," B-Girl pointed at her home girl's RX-7 with the kit, big spoiler, and 5 stars on it. "The Pink Panther" was written in hot pink on the front tag.

"What's good bitch!" B-Girl hopped out the front seat and walked around the car to give her friend a hug.

"My main bitch!!!" Princess was hype. Chuck checked her out and was immediately turned on. She was a slim goody, a cute red-bone. Her curves were small but she had a gap between her legs that stood out; that monkey was calling his name.

"This is C-Roy right here bitch. He got that shit!"

"How you doing?" Princess extended her hand. She spoke real ghetto and southern, sounding like a hood rat.

"I'm good ma."

"Come on ya'll let's head inside and get this party started," B-Girl walked off and the two followed closely behind.

****

"Hey baby! I missed you, where you been?" Grandma asked hugging CeCe tightly.

"Hey, I missed you too. I've been staying with my friend," CeCe answered.

She walked around and hugged her family one by one and embraced all of the love. After her little argument with Chuck, this was just what she needed. Neither she nor her Aunt said anything about what had just happened. They all laughed and talked and started having a good time. Good food, good laughs, and family for the holidays. She was in total bliss.

****

Chuck tried his first one on one and the moment the cocaine hit his nose, the burning sensation made him cough heavily and place the bill on the table. The cocaine ran quickly through his veins and took over. Never had he experienced such a feeling; he didn't know that this was the feeling he would wind up chasing forever. He was hooked after his first hit and didn't know it.

The girls passed the bill back and forth as the NWA album blasted through the radio. The music, alcohol, and drugs took over all of them. The girls started getting hot and decided to strip down to their panties and bra. Chuck stripped down to his boxers. They looked at that dick and knew it was about to go down.

"Here, sit back on the couch," B-Girl instructed as he leaned back. She whipped out his dick, spread some blow across it, and sniffed it off. She licked up the residue. She stuck it in her mouth and began working it, as Princess sat on his face and he began nibbling away at her clit.

He was giving and getting some five star head as B-Girl played in her hairy pussy, sloshing the juices around as his dick grew in her mouth. Princess hopped off his face and joined her friend as she licked his balls while B-Girl sucked, then they switched.

Chuck didn't know if it was the cocaine making him feel like this, or his ménage' tois, but his dick was harder than a missile. It didn't have any feeling though, it was numb. However the slob game kept him up. Princess sunk his big dick deep in her pussy and moaned. "Oh shit," as she began to jump up and down on the dick like she was riding a horse. His dick was hitting the right spot and Princess was going to work as B-girl played with his balls. She jumped up and B-Girl spread that ass apart doggy style on the couch. Chuck started tearing that ass up with long, deep strokes. "You like dis dick don't you bitch?" Chuck spat between thrusts.

"Yes daddy, fuck me!" B-Girl screamed as Chuck drilled that ass from the back, occasionally taking his dick out to shove it down Princess's throat. He was tearing both their asses up and the cocaine was making him feel like a porno stud. Not once did it cross his mind that he had just met these hoes, and not once did he think about wearing a condom.

The consequences of your actions seldom enter the mind when you are having fun. He didn't even think about his welcome hit to cocaine, or think about his addiction that was building on the low. Thanksgiving 1992 was the beginning of a new drug habit and the beginning of his downfall. It felt so good. How could something that felt so right be so wrong? This was a turning point in Chuck's life and from this day forward he would never be the same.

Chapter 19

The sun began to work its way through the blinds and the alarm clock blared letting CeCe know that Monday morning had finally come and her tears finally began to dry up. Seeing Chuck with that girl when he should have been picking her up from downtown really tore her up the last few days. Chevella and her grandmother tried to console her, but her heart was invested in Chuck.

She was in love with Chuck, but when he hurt her feelings, she turned to Kevin for emotional support. Kevin was more of a good man than Chuck, but Chuck was the bad boy that CeCe couldn't get out of her system. In her eyes nobody understood what she was going through and the talks Chevella gave her over the weekend fell upon deaf ears.

CeCe fought the urge to stay in the bed and she wrestled herself from the grip of her plush comforter and the warmth that held onto her throughout the night. Once the cold air rushed her bones, she flicked on her heater and headed to the bathroom to wash up. She made sure she grabbed two different color wash cloths this time because the last time she used the same color code was the day that changed her life forever.

She turned the water on and let the heat steam up the bathroom as she pinned up her hair in the mirror and applied a Noxzema mask to her face. She stepped in the shower and let the hot water knock the chill off of her bones. As she began to bathe, she thought about what her next move was going to be. She knew her daddy slid her some stacks to get a whip, so she figured she would throw a down payment on a car and do some shopping.

After she finished getting herself together, she picked up the house phone and dialed up Kevin.

"Hello," he answered with the radio pumping in the background wit some unknown rock and roll loud in her ear.

"I guess that's his white side coming out," CeCe told herself. She demanded, "Turn that music down. Dang, I can't even hear myself think."

"My bad," he turned the music down and returned to the line, "What's up with you? You feeling better about the family dispute that upset you this weekend?"

"Yeah, I feel better thanks to you. I need a favor from you today."

"What you need?"

"I need a ride to go and get a car after school today. Can you take me?" she asked in the sweetest seductive tone she could muster up while admiring herself in the mirror.

"Sure, I can do that. We don't have practice today. You going to buy a car yourself?"

"Yes," she blurted with an attitude, "I'm almost eighteen you know."

"Almost, but you're not there yet, so how you gone pull that off?"

"My daddy knows somebody and he has somebody on the outside that's handling everything. All I have to do is go pay the money and I'm driving off the lot."

"Wow, who's your dad? It sounds like he is a powerful man to be able to do things like that from jail"

"I really don't know myself anymore, but I just want a car so I'm not asking a million questions I don't care about. So you gon' to take me or what?" she spoke with attitude rearing its ugly head.

Kevin knew better than to get her started and submitted, "Yeah, I'll take you. I'll be there after school to pick you up. I'm gon' leave a little early so I can be there when you get out."

The biggest smile ever crept across CeCe's lips as she still admired herself in the mirror. She felt like she had won a battle, but she concealed it and answered calmly, "Thanks. I'll see you then."

She hung up the phone, put the finishing touches on herself, and headed out the door to get this school day over with.

****

Chuck was up early before the sun came up because the traffic that was coming though the spot was heavy. He always had Blaze on twenty four hour watch since he couldn't sleep because of his habit. On this morning, Blaze had finally crashed like any other drug addict. People came directly upstairs to Chuck's crib and he hadn't been to sleep. His new coke habit had him up all night; he was on the verge of going days without sleep.

He spent his morning cooking up ounces to keep the money flowing. By the time the sun reached his blinds, he had made $6,000. While all the regular kids were on their way to school, Chuck was counting paper. The banks and pawn shops opened up around nine, so he made sure he had enough dope on deck to make more. Since him and CeCe got into it at the BP the other day, he hadn't talked to her and he really hadn't thought about the situation again. The money never stopped, and B-Girl and Princess stayed on his mind.

He experienced his first threesome and his first time trying coke in the same night. He was turned out and really hadn't slept all weekend. The constant flow of money made the time go by quickly and it was noon before he knew it. Chuck had turned the trap into a gold mine and from being around all weekend he saw how much his operation had grown.

The knock at the door was familiar one; Chuck knew it was his relief. He opened it with the quickness, "Damn nigga, you been sleep since yesterday. I ain't even been to sleep, but I've been making lots of money."

"I know, shit I was tired. You look tired and I need me something to wake me up so what we working with?"

"You already know what we working with. You know it ain't nothing but the truth when I cook it up Blood. When a head say I got this from C-Roy, they know they getting nothing but the best."

"True that, well let me get a hit of that good shit!"

Chuck went into the room and grabbed an ounce because he knew he was ready to crash and get some sleep. It had been a long weekend and now that his high was descending he kept thinking about CeCe. He figured he would get some rest and catch up with her after school or something.

****

Kevin pulled into the parking lot early as he said he would and he saw Erica walking out of the building. He pulled up on her and rolled his window down to speak.

"Hey Erica!"

Erica turned around, startled that anybody even knew her at this school. She recognized the smile instantly, "Hey Kevin!!! What are you doing up here? Ain't you supposed to be in school right now?" she walked up and stuck her elbows in the window.

"I left early to come and get CeCe; she's supposed to be getting a car."

"Say word? She getting a car and haven't even called me?" she asked hating on the low and digging Kevin the whole time.

"Hey, my name Bennett, and I ain't in it. What you doing up here anyway?"

"I had to come and bring my lil cousin something important. I'm about to get out of here cause I have somewhere to be. Get a pen and paper and take my number down. Call me later on; I want to talk to you about something."

"Aight," he answered taking her number. He didn't think anything about her giving him the number, but he hurried up and tucked it away. He figured he would forget to mention that he had even seen her because he knew how CeCe jumped to conclusions about everything.

With her being the first black girl he had actually been with, he was definitely stuck on her. But all that going black and not going back was some bullshit; it was too many sexy white girls that turned him on too. He was looking to try on a few other races before it was all said and done. He knew when college started; he was going to have all the women as a star quarterback.

CeCe came prancing out and opened the truck door interrupting his thoughts, "Hey you!"

"Hey Baby, you feeling better?" he asked right before his lips greeted hers.

"Yeah, I'm feeling better. I was sick earlier and throwing up, but after that I was cool. I've been crying a lot and stressed, so that's probably it," she spoke with her lips but her mind was saying, "*I been sick a lot lately and I haven't come on my period yet.*"

CeCe was very guarded with her life, so she wasn't open with the things that went on with her. Even knowing that Kevin could be the reason for her sickness, she chose not to share it. If her dad taught her one thing when she was little, it was that her business was her business and she needed to keep it to herself. Yeah she would tell her girls everything, but she only told dudes what they wanted to hear.

"Where we going?"

"My dad gave me this address," she handed him a piece of paper, "I think it's on the south side."

"Yeah, I think I know where this is. I got you. You hungry?" he asked as he was driving off.

"Yeah, stop by the lil soul food joint on 311. I don't really want no fast food."

"Aight bet."

****

Blaze's knock on the door awoke Chuck from his deep sleep on the couch. His first reaction was to grab the gun on the table, but he sat it back down. He looked at the time and he saw he only had two hours of sleep, so the trap was officially booming.

"Wassup Blood," Chuck opened the door stretching.

"Man it's been rolling! I need some more shit. That's the shit that killed Elvis right there. I need another one," Blaze sang wide eyed and sweating like a runaway slave.

"Where my money at? First things first."

Blaze handed him a wad of bills some crumpled up, some of them fresh. It didn't matter to Chuck either way, as long as it tallied up to sixteen hundred they were good. All the product Blaze had been moving for him should have set his pockets straight, but he smoked up every piece of his profit and could barely keep the water and lights on in his crib. He was forever borrowing money from Chuck, but he didn't care because he always got it back and then some.

There was a knock on the door while he was in the back and Blaze hollered out, "I got it!" so he didn't lose his focus. He counted every dollar and noticed it was thirty dollars short, but he didn't trip because he was getting over anyway. He grabbed another ounce and headed back to the living room to pass it off.

"Where you come from?" Chuck asked B-Girl when he came around the corner.

"You wasn't answering the phone, so I decided to swoop through. What you up to?"

Chuck handed the crack to Blaze and let him out before he answered, "Shit, just grinding like I always do. Shouldn't you be doing the same?"

"Yeah, I need to re-up, but I just came to chill with you. Is that ok?"

"Yeah that's cool. I see you brought beer," he peeked in the bag she brought.

"Yep, so you know what it is. Where the good shit at?"

"I got it in the room. You might as well come in here so we can chill and watch *Boyz in the Hood*."

"That's wassup. I want to get comfortable anyway," B-Girl said as she stood up and climbed her way out of her shirt and peeled her tights off. She was in her tank top and thongs.

Chuck's dick definitely noticed that ass swaying as she walked into the room and his boxers began to expose the hard on that was creeping up on him. She lay across the bed like a tiger while he put in the VHS tape and pressed play. There was no need in playing, so he went ahead and fixed up the bill so she could get started. The dark curtains made his room feel like it was later than what it was. *"It's about to go down in here,"* he thought as he passed her the bill.

****

"Ohhhhh, I love this car!!!!" CeCe shouted as she sat in the Honda Accord and sucked in that new car smell. She test drove it and it drove like a dream. She had wanted one of these cars for years and her heart was fluttering at the fact that her dad already had it picked out for her. He took care of everything, so all she had to do was say yes and let the dealer swipe her card to take care of the agreed upon down payment. Everything after that was set up for automatic draft.

"Now you can come to see me at night when my mom goes to work," Kevin snuck in with a smile.

"That's right boo. I can come see you. If you ever need me to come and get you all you have to do is call me."

"Yeah, if you're ever at home for me to call. You're always gone every time I call."

"I know and I need to buy a beeper so I can keep up with everybody, especially since I'm rolling now."

"I'm scared of you! What you about to get into? I have to go so I can get to the library and meet my group to work on this project."

"I'm about to go to the mall and do some shopping. Thanks again," she hugged him and gave him a passionate kiss.

Chapter 20

His suit was crisp, freshly starched and definitely tailored to his body. It was jet black, with gleaming white pen stripes. It ran in a straight line on top of a bright white collared shirt, with a tie that matched the stripes on the jacket and a matching handkerchief in his jacket pocket. Jesús was definitely clean, with the black and white gators to match his suit. This city had never seen a gangster like this in person. Mexico was his home, and he proudly repped it. The only reason he was in the states was to come and have a sit down with his number one man, Vernon White.

His badge and credentials read Jackie Jones, the lawyer that visited Vernon the first time, and he was a spitting image of him. Jackie Jones was a black man, but he looked almost exactly like Jesús Martinez, the leader of the Dragon Cartel. He was the head of the body and the leader of the team. One of the most dangerous men in Mexico just stepped inside the Forsyth County Jail to talk to a man who helped him build his empire from the ground up.

The officers cleared him and nobody had an idea who was there. Vernon admitted to the murders to cover up for his son. Regardless who his son murdered, he wasn't serving time in a hick ass town like this.

He was led into a room for attorneys and clients, with no outside sound. He looked around at the old cruddy jail system they had and knew that the murder in Miami would set Vernon free. It was only a matter of time, but Vernon seemed like he couldn't do the time.

He was seated and as soon as the door shut behind him, the conversation began.

"Que pasa amigo," Jesús spoke, extending his hand, "Long time no see."

"Que pasa," he embraced his leader, "Thank you for coming. I'm going to cut to the chase. The problem that we sent T-Bone and Chico to eliminate actually eliminated them. I went to murder him afterwards myself, but I got call from my daughter, she had just been beaten at school. I rushed to the hospital to make sure she was fine, where I came face to face with our problem. I sent Hakeem to murder him, but he took Hakeem out. My daughter met him and fell for him by some unlucky coincidence. He ended up spending the night at my house. So I went to murder his mom to send a message and break him down, but he won't break. He's got some connect in the projects and he's making money and becoming a threat. On top of that, my baby girl is in love with him, so his death would crush her. I love my daughter, but I love my team as well. Chuck has to die, just make sure my daughter doesn't die with him. I need to get out of here Jesús, my little girl is caught in the middle of a drug war and she doesn't even know it. I gotta be the one to pull my baby away from him because she's still trying to be with him. He can't die until I look him in his eyes, you owe me that much. I'm going to save my baby girl," Vernon recited and didn't blink. He had been thinking about what to say since he found out Jesús was visiting him.

"Ok, we'll get you out. He will die and you will do it. We're going to take these streets back and these wanna be gangsters who are trying not to buy from us, and finding new connects are all gonna die. This town is too fucking small for some lil nigga to be killing big niggas in my organization. T-Bone and Chico were worth money to me and your daughter's fucking boyfriend is the reason I'm losing $200,000 a month," Jesús calmly said. His eyes were bitter and his face showed no emotion.

****

Chuck Jenkins woke up that morning with his mother cooking breakfast while he got dressed for school. His mother was sober and clean that morning and performing her motherly duties. He and his mom talked and laughed and had a great morning before he left for school. He stopped by the store to grab some gum, but saw T-Bone and Chico inside and he went on to school.

Chuck met CeCe and it threw a monkey wrench in the program. The plan was to kill Chuck the same day they left for lunch. The hit was called off since CeCe was in the car, so Chuck got a pass. He and his friends murdered T-Bone and Chico and thought they were going to get away. Vernon saw the boys flee from the scene because he was outside waiting for Chuck's body. He paid Hakeem to murder Chuck, but Chuck murdered him instead. Harold and Tony were hired right after that and the two of them are still missing. Precious even had her brains blown out with some dude she enlisted to help her. Chuck had turned out to be one slippery snake, but that's what happens when you send boys to do a man's job. Vernon couldn't wait to get his hands on him.

****

"You will be out by summer, I can promise you that. You have to take care of this problem and then report back down to Atlanta. Chevella is here and is going to take care of CeCe for a while. You can rest my friend, peace will come to you." Jesús said with his accent hanging on every word. He wasn't a man of many words and had said all that needed to be said. They exchanged goodbyes and he was on his way back to Mexico.

****

CeCe finished up her shopping and decided to grab something sexy out of Victoria's Secret to go and surprise Chuck. She kept finding herself walking around craving this and that and she ate a little bit of everything. She packed her bags in the trunk and hopped in her new whip feeling a new found freedom. Regardless of the fact that she had a new car, she still had to go to school because that remained a top priority.

She decided that she didn't want to stop by the pay phone to call ahead because she still had her key to get in. The entire way to Chuck's she thought about jumping up and down on his magic stick. She needed to make up with him and she was willing to let the whole BP incident go.

CeCe pulled up to the house and parked behind Chuck's car, grabbed the Victoria's Secret bag out the back and locked up the car. The crack heads lingering around outside with Blaze had that, "I'll steal your shit" look. She knew Chuck wasn't having that, but she didn't want to take any chances. She made her way into the breezeway and up the steps to Chuck's door.

She slid the key in the hole, unlocked the bottom lock, twisted the knob and noticed the top lock was on. As she was inserting the key in the hole she paused. She stuck her ear to the door and listened to what was going on inside. There was music playing, and she was sure she heard the sounds of lovemaking.

"What the fuck?" she said to herself as she turned the key and the knob slowly and eased the door open. The sound beat on her ear drums clearly "Uhhh, Uhhh, Oh shit Daddy lick this pussy!" causing tears to go on a roller coaster ride down her cheeks soaking into her shirt.

She stepped inside with her feelings devastated and getting worse with each erotic moan that hummed from the back room. This is not what she came over for, but her emotions were making her think crazy thoughts. She thought about sliding into the kitchen, grabbing a butcher knife and slicing and dicing him and whatever bitch he was with. *"Nah, fuck that, I know exactly what I'm about to do,"* she said to herself as she calmly left just as easily as she came in. She didn't let the door make any noise to disturb what was going on. She ran to the car with the wind and misty rain adding to her tears. She snatched the door open, hopped in, and took off heading home. The car hit two wheels as she hit the curb flying like a bat out of hell. Her mind raced, and curse words flew from her mouth as she raced to her grandmothers' house.

****

"Oh fucccccckkkkkkkk," B-Girl gripped Chuck's head clamping her legs tightly as her body shook while she came all in his mouth. He kept licking and didn't mind her restraint.

Chuck finally was released from her kung fu grip and while she was laying there shaking he kindly slid her to the edge of the bed and placed her feet on his shoulders. He positioned himself with his hands on the bed and eased inside of her. "Damn baby, this pussy wet," he assured her as he began to work his way inside of her. He didn't waste any time synthesizing his movements or establishing a steady stroke.

"Oh baby yes, fuck that pussy baby," B-Girl clamped her hands around his neck as he began to pound on her pussy faster and harder with each stroke. She began moaning uncontrollably with him humping her like a horse; she threw it back like a porno star.

Chuck was lost inside of her and deeply digging her out when he thought he heard footsteps rushing towards his room. Before he knew what was even going on, he looked up and saw the chrome shining in the dark. His heart skipped a beat and B-Girl screamed...

****

"Muthafucka you gon' play me like this!" CeCe bellowed with Chevella's .380 pistol. She stole it from under the seat of her car and had it between both hands, aimed directly at Chuck.

The limited amount of light produced by the red bulb made CeCe look much scarier in the dark hallway and the light beams exposed her trail of tears streaming her cheeks. Chuck snatched his dick out of the pussy and stood erect at the side of bed while B-Girl was frozen with fear. CeCe's silhouette was gangsta, but did she have it in her to pull the trigger?

"Baby, it's not what it looks like," Chuck's voice trembled more than his body, but miraculously his dick was still rock hard.

"Oh really? So you telling me this bitch ain't in here and yo hard dick wasn't in her wack ass pussy?" CeCe spit back like venom.

"Baby wait, please, I can explain."

"You can explain that?" she aimed the gun at his genitals, "Go 'head then Chuck. Explain that shit."

CeCe stood back looking at a scared shitless, butt ass naked Chuck. She glanced over at B-Girl, *"Damn, this bitch got a bad ass body,"* she thought. She then looked back over at Chuck's soldier still standing at full attention. The moistness of her panties was an indicator that she was definitely turned on by his big dick, and her sexy ass body. Even though her mind was changing about what she planned to do, her actions didn't show it and she was eager to hear him out. "I'm listening," she spoke calmer, with anticipation dancing on her vocal cords.

"Baby, I can't even explain it. Fuck it. You caught me. I fucked up. I'm sorry." All of those short sentences managed to escape Chuck's mouth as he searched for something better to say. His dick began to lose stiffness and descend back towards his thighs. *"Fuck it, she caught me,"* was the only rationalization that came to mind. His heart was pounding in his chest while standing there looking down the barrel of the gun waiting for the firing to commence.

This was the moment of truth for her, CeCe knew it was time to make a decision and she figured she would do the best thing possible in a situation like this. She stepped slowly into the room surveying the two and with each little step she took, Chuck took little steps backwards. B-Girl lay still as a rock as she walked over and looked into her eyes. She reached one hand out and wiped it across her juice box soaking her finger, while she still had the gun pointed at Chuck.

"What the fuck is this crazy bitch doing," B-Girl thought as she took in CeCe's face and remembered her from the BP. She even recognized the gun stuck to her left hand pointed at Chuck. *"Oh shit, that's that sexy bitch from the BP,"* her mind kept rationalizing what was going on, but what she saw was shocking the shit out of her.

CeCe took her finger and tasted the sweet juices, then laid the pistol on the dresser and peeled her shirt off exposing her succulent breasts sitting nicely in the lace bra she wore. She then unbuttoned her pants and dropped them to the floor. B-Girl caught on that she was about to join the fun and was already on her knees on the bed rubbing her soft hands on her. "Ummmmmm," she moaned as Chuck began to walk closer.

"Hell yeah Baby," Chuck said as he walked up and began to rub on the front of her body, while B-Girl rubbed on her back. CeCe grabbed his dick and began to massage it as B-Girl popped her bra releasing the twins from bondage. Chuck bent over and took her left nipple between his teeth and began to suck.

"Oh yes," CeCe released the backed up frustration and submitted to the tongues lashing her body with pleasurable strokes as "Just Chill" by Guy played on the radio. Chuck and B-girl devoured her body as he sucked on her nipples and she licked up and down her back.

B-Girl played in her wet snatch and gave her the dip and sniff test to make sure the pussy was fresh. There was not even the slightest fragrance. That was her green light to join Chuck in the front of CeCe's body while she spread her legs giving access to the clit. B-Girl sucked that fat clit while Chuck rubbed on her body.

The three of them were engulfed in a love triangle and it was getting hotter by the minute. Moans, ooh's, and ahh's all bounced from their lips simultaneously. CeCe's first ménage was beginning wonderfully and she interrupted what was going on to climb onto the bed as B-Girl dove back in between her legs and Chuck straddled her face and fed her his meat. Sucking on him while B-Girl was licking the clit pleased her beyond her imagination. The whole scene was exciting her so much. She began to wind her hips as dick was being shoveled into her mouth and she felt a tingling sensation. She was about to cum harder than she ever had before. Just when her body was about to explode with pleasure…

"CeCe!!! What the fuck is going on in here!!!" Chevella screamed at the sight of the threesome.

All three faces looked up and their expressions read *"OH SHIT!!!!"*…

To Be Continued…

Sneak Peek into Broken Mirrors

<u>PROLOGUE</u>

"What's taking CeCe so long to get here? She should have been here by now," Chevella paced the floor, growing aggravated talking to Vernon's mother, who is not her mother.

"I don't know where that child is, her father just got her a new car, and she is a teenager now, and she deserves the truth," Ms. Ethel hissed at Chevella.

Chevella and Ms. Ethel had been having problems since before CeCe was born. Like the whole situation was her fault, and Tonya and Vernon were just both innocent, "So what you want me to do? Just tell her everything she had known up until now has all been a lie?"

"She's a big girl now, and she can handle it. Her lil fast ass running around just like ya'll did with my son years ago, and I caught her in the act with a boy in the house just like I did the 3 of you!" Ms. Ethel pointed her old, crumpled finger at Chevella, and it made her drift back to when she caught them in the act.

****

Chevella lay flat on her belly on the plush, king size bed that sat in the middle of Vernon's room, while her sister lay next her gazing into her eyes. Tonya was beautiful, damn near perfect image of Chevella, which was the reason they even called themselves sisters in the first place. They looked so much alike as far as their curvy figures, flawless skin, and beautiful faces, but they were indeed two different people and had no blood running in between them, only the man that sat on his knees between them, caressing them both softly.

Vernon linked the two of them together at a party one night, and it had been on ever since. The two women fell in love with each other's looks, just as if they were primping themselves in the mirror at home. They looked like twins, and he knew he had to have the two of them. His appetite wouldn't be complete without these two women in his life.

"Hey, me and my girl noticed you come in from across the room, and we wanted to meet you," Vernon smiled flashing his pearly whites, mesmerizing her with his hazel brown eyes. He was one of the most handsome men she had laid eyes on this little crappy country town that her mother moved to 2 years ago for a job with RJ Reynolds, one of the leading tobacco companies in Winston-Salem, NC. His afro was tight, and the burgundy bell bottoms along with the white pizza collared shirt really made him look like a pimp. His collars hung from the shirt as big as a NY slice of pizza, crisp, and his shirt was silk with only the bottom button closed exposing his chest and nicely chiseled abs. The only thing she couldn't get over was the fact that he had a girl.

"Hi," Chevella reached out and accepted Vernon's firm, but soft hands, "Nice to meet you. Is that your girl over there smiling?" she nodded towards Tonya sitting on the couch cheesing hard.

"Yeah, that's her. How about you come over so I can introduce the two of you?"

"Ummm, I'm just now getting here and I want to at least speak to a few folks I know around the room. How about I just catch back up to the two of you later?"

"That's fine, but make sure you stop through so I can introduce the two of you. As you can see, the two of you look like sisters," Vernon pointed out only what Chevella had been thinking this entire time.

To make a long story short, the two women fell in love with each other since they were already in love with themselves. The two of them face to face was like looking into a mirror, with Vernon standing behind them smiling from ear to ear. Their bodies even curved the same, only difference was Chevella's ass, hips, and thighs spread further than Tonya's. They couldn't wait to get with each other, and there they all were from that first night.

The memories of how they met played in their heads, as Vernon's dick was being stroked by the two women. He was in heaven as he sat up on his knees, rubbing and caressing these two beauties as they stroked his manhood the full ten inches. With thick, long dick pulsating between the women's finger tips, Vernon couldn't take just being stroked, and headed straight for Chevella's mouth.

She immediately took as much of him as she could, while Tonya made her way to juggle his balls with her tongue. Vernon was in heaven, and this night couldn't have been any better. As he stroked both of their heads full of hair, he just enjoyed looking at the fact that he had duplicated his one love, Tonya. He was in heaven until the door busted open, light flicked on, and his mother's finger pointed at the three of them and yelled,

"What in the hell you doing with these two whores in my house!!"

****

"Well if you feel like she needs to know that bad, why don't you tell her? Why you always want somebody else to do your dirty work for you. Tell her, it makes no difference to me." Chevella said nonchalantly still pacing back and forth.

"She never made a difference to you, that's why we are in this position that we are in. All the lies and deceit that surrounds that baby's life, I wouldn't be surprised if she was running around like ya'll all used to, who knows? What goes around comes around."

"Look, I don't need to keep being chastised by you for some shit I done years ago. The past is the past, and I'm over it, you need to get your head back in the game old lady. You too old to be acting like you used to back then."

"Ok past is the past," Ms. Ethel started giving up trying to reason with Chevella. She was still just as bull headed and disrespectful as she was when they were kids. She still had the same snotty attitude like no one could tell her anything. "Well, we'll see how CeCe takes knowing that her mother wasn't even her." She started, but was interrupted by the phone ringing. Maybe God was trying to tell her to leave it alone, and let them sort this mess out themselves. She reached for the phone, placed it to her ear, and spoke in a calm tone, "Hello?"

To Be Continued

About The Author

Mike O was born and raised on the streets of Winston-Salem, NC. His whole young life was spent making the wrong choices and following a path that is all too familiar that he resurrects in his debut novel "1000 Grams" in hopes of his testimony to reach a young soul lost to help them find their way back. This gritty street tale will you take you through the good, the bad, and the ugly of Mike O's past. Since his first release, he went on to pen a short story trilogy entitled "Fakebook Chronicles" Vol.1, 2, and 3. Recently signing on with D.C. Bookdiva Publications, he plans to keep the heat coming, so be on the lookout for more titles by this new author!

DC BOOKDIVA PUBLICATIONS

SECRETS

Love, Betrayal, and Revenge

NEVER DIE

EYONE WILLIAMS

National Best Selling Author of Lorton Legends

In Stores and Ereaders Now!

Dark Secrets Begin

"Who did it, Niya? Who pulled the trigger?"

I rolled my eyes at the detective and sighed. He was getting on my fucking nerves asking me the same damn question in different ways after I had already told him I ain't know shit about the murder in front of my apartment building. So what I saw the whole thing go down? Shit like that went down all the time in my hood. It wasn't any of my business, and the streets of D.C. had schooled me well—I knew how to mind my damn business. I had seen too many people who opened their mouth about something that had nothing to do with them turn up missing.

The white detective glared at me and said, "What if that was your brother or cousin out there dead, for no reason? Would you still know nothing, as you say, young lady?"

I yawned, tired from hanging out all night at the go-go. "I can't tell you what I don't know. Sorry." I shrugged. I was ready to get the fuck on about my business.

The detective sighed with frustration. He shook his head knowing he was going to get no info out of me. "Come on, I know somebody outside saw something. Nobody can keep a secret in the streets."

Pissed off, I sucked my teeth and said, "Look, man, I don't know shit. I ain't see shit. How many times I gotta tell you that?" I shook my head and looked at my Gucci watch. It was 2:37 p.m. It was definitely time to roll.

Fed up, the detective walked over to the thick wooden door, opened it, and said, "I'm done for now. You can go."

He ain't have to tell me twice. I was out of there.

Once downstairs, I called my sister Jasmine and asked her to come get me from the police headquarters, where the homicide branch was located. Jasmine told me she was on her way. I shut my phone and sighed. Jasmine was always there for me, like Johnnie-on-the-spot.

Jasmine was my heart. At 25, she was seven years older than I was. However, she had been my sister/guardian since I was 14. On the real, she raised me. Our mother was sentenced to twenty-two years in federal prison in 2002 for serving an undercover one hundred and fifty grams of crack. Our father was a street legend in D.C., or so I was told. He came up with the likes of Michael "Fray" Salters and Eddie Mathis. I had heard so many stories about my father, Marvin Truman. He was shot to death in 1991, when I was only 5 years old. I never got over that. Nevertheless, life goes on. Moms held it down like a true soldier, doing whatever she had to do. Back then I didn't know that meant moving coke to take care of me and Jasmine, until I saw it on the news after the feds raided our Silver Spring, Maryland, home. Shit really hit the fan after that. Moms was sent off to federal prison. The feds took everything we had. Me and Jasmine moved back to the hood, our real home—uptown D.C. We had lived everywhere: Garfield Terrace, 10th and W, Kennedy Street, and Georgia Avenue. We got an apartment on Georgia Avenue and Rittenhouse Street, in Northwest.

From then on, Jasmine made sure we were well taken care of—by any means.

A short while later, Jasmine pulled up in her white Range Rover. She sat behind the wheel in a pair of black Prada shades, fly as shit. As always, her hair was freshly done and her gear was top of the line: Gucci this, Fendi that. Her cute face and golden-brown skin looked just like mine—we got it from moms.

I jumped in the Range, and we pulled off into traffic. It was warm outside, so I put the window down and let the wind blow in my face for a second.

Moving through traffic, Jasmine said, "So what was they asking you up in there?"

"Regular bullshit—who did it, what did I see, and all that." I looked down at my vibrating cell phone and saw that it was this dude named Face. He was cool, but I decided to call him back later. Didn't really feel like talking.

Heading up 7th Street, Jasmine asked, "What did you tell them peoples?"

"I told them I ain't know shit. What else was I gon' tell them?" I said that with a little attitude. Jasmine knew me better than to ask me some shit like that. I ain't fuck with no cops.

My sister smiled at my response. "Did they bring up Jay's name?"

"Nah, they ain't bring up his name at all."

Jay was the one who really did the killing the cops were asking me about. Talk had it that Jay smoked this dude named Tyriq because Tyriq kicked in the door of his apartment and stole $50,000. By the way, Jay was also my sister's man. He was well respected in the streets of D.C. He was cool as shit, and. I had a lot of love for him. On top of that, my mother used to deal with him way back in the day, so it made him cool long before he started messing with Jasmine. On everything, Jay was a fly nigga, a real uptown nigga who was about his paper. And he was willing to do everything in his power to protect it. He was dangerous. He would smoke a nigga in the blink of an eye, like it wasn't shit.

"Niggaz ain't crazy," I said. "Ain't nobody gon' say shit about him to the police."

Jasmine sighed. "Don't believe that. Niggaz out here are snakes—they'll tell on they mother to get out of going to prison."

I laughed. "Ain't that the truth."

Jasmine smirked, "Yeah, but he ain't to be fucked with."

Her phone rang. She checked the number and answered it. From the sound of the conversation, I could it was Jay. She was telling him about my visit to the homicide branch. Her conversation with him was short and sweet. She ended the call with him, looked at me, and said, "Jay said you did good, said you a good girl." She winked at me and laughed.

I rolled my eyes and blushed. Growing up, I had a little crush on Jay's fine ass, but I would never cross my sister like that and fuck her man. That wasn't in my blood. Blood was always thicker than water. That's how my mother raised us.

"I hope the police don't keep pressin' me 'bout that shit."

"Don't worry about it, Niya. They'll be investigating another murder in a day or two. Don't even trip. Shit will blow over. Plus, you wasn't the only one outside that night."

Her words comforted me. She'd had that kind of effect on me ever since I was a little girl.

As if I didn't know any better, Jasmine said, "Niya, I don't want you talkin' to nobody about that shit that went down. Okay?"

I sucked my teeth and caught a little attitude about that shit. "Come on, Jaz, you know damn well I know how to keep my mouth shut. Miss me with that bullshit. I ain't no little girl."

Jasmine laughed. "My bad. Oh, I forgot you 18 now. You all grown up now."

I couldn't be mad at her for joking about my age; in reality, she had treated me like I was grown since I was, like, 14. Coming up, she let me learn on my own, but she still made sure she taught me how shit really went too. She taught me how to be tough, take care of myself, how to recognize game niggaz spit, how to survive in the mean streets, and how to never let a motherfucker get out on me. Moms had taught her the same shit.

"Niya, who all was outside when Tyriq got shot?"

I told Jasmine it was me, two of my girlfriends, and a few niggaz from around the way. I named them all. I was sure she would pass the information on to Jay for safe keeping.

We pulled up in front of our building on Rittenhouse Street. A few street dudes were standing across the street by the alley doing their thing. Hustling was all they knew. Me and Jasmine were always safe and comfortable around the way. Everybody knew us; we were like family to them. Jasmine parked behind Jay's royal-blue Bentley GT. Jay was leaning against the car smoking weed and talking on his cell phone. He had on a white T-shirt, blue jeans, and black Jordans. The diamonds in his chain and the big one in his pinky ring stood out, making it clear that he was getting more money than most niggaz on the block. He had sexy, smooth dark skin—that shit that drove the ladies crazy in the streets. When he smiled, his bright white teeth made him look even finer. He kept his hair cut low, with thick waves. His swagger was full-blown. His right-hand man, Troy, was sitting inside the Bentley counting money. A few dudes who looked up to Jay were nearby. Everybody loved being around Jay.

Jay ended his call and smiled at me as I stepped out of the Range. I was looking good as shit in my Seven jeans. I nodded at Jay and said, "What's up?"

He slipped his phone in his pocket and went in his other pocket and pulled out a handful of fifties and hundreds—all big faces. He handed me damn near a thousand and said, "Here, Niya, take this and hit the mall. Treat yourself, baby girl. I fucks with you; I like how you keep your mouth closed." He winked.

"You know what it is," I smiled. "I mind my business. Good lookin', though." I stuffed the money in my Gucci bag. That was my reward for not saying a word to the police about what I saw.

Jasmine came around the truck with her arms folded. The look on her face made it clear that she had an attitude with Jay, which was wild because she was just talking to him like everything was all good. I figured that the attitude must have been about some shit from earlier. That was none of my business.

Jay looked at Jasmine and smiled. "Why you actin' like that, boo?"

"Don't 'boo' me, nigga." Jasmine rolled her eyes and shifted all of her weight to her right leg, looking real hood.

I started to wonder what was up with them. They didn't do too much beefin'.

Jay slid up on Jasmine real smooth, put his arm around her, and walked her down the block as they talked about whatever was going on.

While that was going down, Troy stepped out of the Bentley and lit a fat-ass Backwood. He took a long pull and blew smoke in the air.

He reminded me of 50 Cent. He was handsome and had the body of a nigga who just came home from prison. One of those niggaz who spent all his time doing push-ups and pull-ups on the inside. He undressed me with his eyes and said, "Damn, Niya, you up in them jeans, baby."

He always flirted with me.

I rolled my eyes and gave him a look like, Whatever, nigga! I couldn't fake, though—I loved the attention from him. But I couldn't be just another piece of pussy to him. If he wanted to get between my legs, it was going to take more than that bullshit he was spittin'. He'd only been home from prison a few months, so I knew he was trying to fuck everything he saw. When he went to prison I was 13, so it was understood that at 18, I was a whole new Niya, with everything in the right places body-wise.

Walking up on me, Troy said, "I see you all grown up now ... lookin' good as shit." He smiled, then licked his lips.

I looked him up and down, put my hand on my hip, and said, "You tell everybody that, don't you?" I thought back to when he used to give me money for the ice cream truck. Now he was trying to fuck me. Niggaz!

"Nah, I don't tell everybody that, but I'm tellin' you that, baby. You a grown woman now from what I can see." He leaned to his left, then his right, looking at my thick hips and thighs.

I tried hard not to blush, but the nigga was laying it on thick.

Troy looked around at the young niggaz on the block and said, "Which one of these young niggaz you fuckin' wit' out here?"

I rolled my eyes and sucked my teeth. "I told you I ain't fuckin' wit' nobody right now," I said, snaking my neck. "Niggaz on some bullshit out here. I got a few friends, though."

Troy licked his lips and said, "Fuck friends. You need a man. I'll do somethin' big wit' your lil' sexy ass. I'll eat that pussy and all that, baby."

I smiled. That made my pussy wet. With the lips he had, I was sure he could eat some pussy like a real pro, but I had to pass. I waved his ass off and said, "Nigga, please, I ain't fuckin' wit' your ass." I stepped off. I could feel his eyes all over me, glued to my ass. I looked back and he was stuck, shaking his head like, Damn, I'll burn her little ass up. I winked at him and headed inside my building.

Jasmine came in behind me. From the look on her face, it seemed like things were cool with her and Jay. I said, "You cool?"

"Yeah, I'm good. Jay just be on some bullshit sometimes."

"You love 'em, though."

"Yeah, I do, but that don't mean he don't get on my damn nerves sometimes."

We made our way inside the apartment. I sat on the sofa and turned on the TV, straight to BET. Jasmine got on the computer and started checking her Facebook page.

"Niggaz always think they slick," she said, eyeing a picture of some girl. "They be too smart for their own good. They be so smart they dumb sometimes. Jay fuckin' this bitch Tish and keep talkin' 'bout it's business and shit, like I'm dumb. He got her makin' runs for him and shit, but ain't no bitch gon' be runnin' around for a nigga that ain't givin' her no money or no dick. I can read between the fuckin' lines."

I got up and went over to the computer to check out the girl. Tish was wearing next to nothing on her Facebook page.

"Oh, that bitch Tish doin' way too much on there." I watched as Jasmine went through Tish's pictures. "Jay fuckin' *her?!*" I asked.

Jasmine "Yeah, Jay fuckin' her, wit' his bitch ass. I don't know what kinda fool he think I am. I know how the game go. I just play along with the shit."

"I'll beat that bitch's ass for you when I see her. She ain't shit."

Jasmine laughed. "Don't trip. I got it under control, boo. But trust and believe Jay ain't the only one that can play that game." She shook her head. "I ain't even gon' trip. Jay pay our rent, he pay the car note on my Range, and he keep me fresh. I stay diggin' in them pockets. Pretty soon we gon' have our own house, and we ain't gon' have to worry about none of these no-good-ass niggaz out here."

I smiled. Jasmine knew how to get what she wanted in life, and I admired that.

Her cell phone rang. She answered it. "Yeah ... okay ... I'ma do it right now. I'll call you when I'm done."

She got up, went to her room, and returned with a brown shopping bag. She set the shopping bag on the kitchen counter. She pulled out a pot and some baking soda, put some water in the pot, and sat it on the stove. She cut the fire on and put some heat under the pot. I was paying close attention. She pulled a brick of powder coke out the shopping bag, cut the wrapper with a knife, and dumped the coke in the pot. After mixing a little baking soda into the pot, she began to work her magic. Our mother taught her how to whip powder into hard white. If the coke was good, Jasmine could turn two bricks of coke into three like it wasn't shit. She had a nice little hustle: She charged $1,000 to turn two bricks into three. A few dudes around the way were moving weight in the coke game but couldn't whip like Jasmine, so they stepped to her to get their shit right.

I watched her work. Even though I didn't fuck around with that shit, I had watched her do her thing long enough to know how to do it myself.

"Jaz, you make that shit look so easy, like you been doin' it all your life," I said.

She laughed. "Ain't shit to it. I been doin' it since I was 'bout 14." She continued to whip the coke with a fork like it was cake batter. "So what's up wit' Troy? I see he been pushin' up on you jive hard."

I rolled my eyes and smirked. "I ain't thinkin' 'bout no damn Troy. He just want some pussy. How old is he anyway?"

"He a year or two older than Jay, so he gotta be 26 or 27. Somethin' like that. He on the come-up, though. If you work your shit, you could have that nigga eatin' out the palm of your hand. You know how the game go, girl."

"Eatin' out the palm of my hand, huh?" I smiled, thinking about how Troy said he'd eat my pussy. Being so much older, I was sure he could suck my pussy dry. That turned me on. No bullshit! "Troy been comin' at me real hard, talkin' that pussy-eatin' shit."

Jasmine smiled and shook her head. "Yeah, Niya, you got his attention. Make that nigga chase you, baby girl. You throw that young pussy on 'em, and he won't know what to do. He just got out too."

I laughed and changed the subject. "We still goin' to see Ma this weekend?"

"Yeah, I hope so," Jasmine said as she finished cooking the first brick. She set it on a plate and put the other one in the pot.

Thinking about my mother made me miss her. We hadn't been to visit her in close to two months. Every time we turned around something new popped up, and we couldn't make it up the road to West Virginia to visit her at Alderson. Still, we stayed in touch with her and took good care of her. Jasmine made sure she did all she could for our mother. Moms wanted for nothing while she did her time.

As the years passed, I grew used to the fact that she was going to be away for a while. I just prayed that she wouldn't have to do the whole twenty-two years the judge gave her. I also grew to hate the system for giving her so much fucking time. Shit, I knew niggaz doing tens and fifteens for smoking niggaz in the streets, but my moms was sitting in on twenty-two years for crack. Bullshit! For real. I had cried myself to sleep so many nights when she first got sentenced. But at the end of the day, it was nothing I could do about the situation but suck it up and be strong. That's the way moms wanted me to be.

There was nothing I wouldn't give to have my moms back in the free world with us. Shit just wasn't the same without her. And all the visits, letters, phone calls, and pictures would never add up to having her free, back with us.

"Ay, Jaz," I said, "I need to get those pictures developed for Ma. I keep forgetting to do it."

Jaz smirked while she was hard at work over the stove. "Not you, Ms. Always On Top of Business."

I laughed. "Shut up, ho. I'ma do it right now, right this minute while we talkin' 'bout it. Let me see your keys."

Jazmin gave me a serious look and said, "Niya, go to the store and bring my shit right back. Don't be all over the city in my shit, showin' off. You know how you get."

I sucked my teeth. "Whatever." Grabbing the keys to the Range off the coffee table, I said, "Ease up, Jaz. I got you. I'll be right back."

I went to my room, grabbed my digital camera, and hit the door.

Order Form

DC Bookdiva Publications

#245 4401-A Connecticut Avenue, NW

Washington, DC 20008

dcbookdiva.com

Name: _____

Inmate ID _____

Address: _____

City/State: _____ **Zip:** _____

QUANTITY	TITLES	PRICE	TOTAL
	Up The Way, Ben	$15.00	
	Dynasty, Dutch	$15.00	
	Dynasty 2, Dutch	$15.00	
	Dynasty 3, Dutch	$15.00	
	Que, Dutch	$15.00	
	Tina, Darrell Debrew	$15.00	
	Trina, Darrell Debrew	$15.00	
	Secrets Never Die, Eyone Williams	$15.00	
	Lorton Legends, Eyone Williams	$15.00	
	The Hustle, Frazier Boy	$15.00	
	A Killer'z Ambition, Nathan Welch	$15.00	
	A Beautiful Satan, RJ Champ	$15.00	

Sub-Total $_____

Shipping/Handling (Via US Media Mail) $3.95 1-2 Books, $7.95 1-3 Books, 4 or more titles-Free Shipping

Shipping $ _____

Total Enclosed $ _____

Certified or government issued checks and money orders, all mail in orders take 5-7 Business days
to be delivered. Books can also be purchased on our website at dcbookdiva.com and by credit card at
1866-928-9990. Incarcerated readers receive 25% discount. Please pay $11.25 per book and apply the same shipping terms as stated above.